ANGEL FLYING TOO CLOSE TO THE GROUND

Annie Garrett

ANGEL FLYING TOO CLOSE TO THE GROUND

WHEELER
PUBLISHING, INC.
ROCKLAND, MA

★ AN AMERICAN COMPANY ★

Published in Large Print by arrangement with
St. Martin's Press in the United States and Canada.

Wheeler Large Print Book Series.

"Angel Flying Too Close to the Ground" words and music by Willie
Nelson copyright © 1979 Full Nelson Music, Inc. All rights
administered by Windswept Pacific Entertainment Co. d/b/a Longitude
Music. All rights reserved. Used by permission. Warner Bros.
Publication U.S. Inc., Miami, FL 33014.

Set in 16 pt. Plantin.

Library of Congress Cataloging-in-Publication Data

Garrett, Annie.
    Angel flying too close to the ground / Annie Garrett.
        p.   cm.—(Wheeler large print book series)
    ISBN 1-56895-382-8 (softcover)
    1. Country musicians—Missouri Branson—Fiction.   2. Women
journalists—United States—Fiction.   3. Country music—Fiction.
4. Branson (Mo.)—Fiction.   5. Large type books.   I. Title.
II. Series.
[PS3557.A71837A84   1996b]
813'.54—dc20
                                                            96-35544
                                                            CIP

For Redstone

CHAPTER ONE

She could remember his eyes. They were gray as this roadway with its gleaming sheen of rain, gray and fringed with blond lashes too long for a boy, too delicate. They were a surprise, those eyes, coming as they did in a face carved sharp as an Ozarks bluff, a face that surmounted a towering frame laced up with long muscles taut as stretched wire. He was even then so heavy-booted and long-limbed and wide-shouldered: powerfully built. But in truth it was his eyes that told his story. What had he been when she had seen him last? Eighteen, maybe nineteen. Yes, nineteen. His eyes were wet that day, and gray as this back road going home.

Tess checked the time on the dashboard clock of her rented Mustang. She was late if she expected to beat Poe, the freelance photographer, into town. They had only just met by phone yesterday, but he had struck her immediately as one of those adhesive types. "I love working as a team," he had told her in a wispy voice that didn't seem properly calibrated to travel the arduous distance of a telephone wire. "I want to see the story with *your* vision, so I can give you the gift of the perfect cover shot." Inwardly, she had groaned; why was it that New Yorkers fastened on career tasks with an intensity that seemed to equate something as frivolous as celebrity journalism with something as complicated and vital as laser brain surgery? True, she, too,

1

brought an intensity to her work as a magazine writer, but she had always secretly known that hers boiled up from a far different source. Her intensity was not solely ambition, not simply an inflated sense of self-worth, not just egomania. If only it were.

For now, she wanted to elude the photographer until it couldn't be delayed any longer. All she wanted was a good hour to herself. An hour would be enough time to return her calls, which she had retrieved from her voice mail—home and office—just before dashing onto the plane at La Guardia. But even with those messages and their degrees of urgency duly noted in her leather Filofax, still, she couldn't bring herself to skirt over and take the highway, a swifter option. Instead, something in her clung to the idea of this country road veined through with tar-patched cracks. A shower had just passed as her plane angled low for landing. The clouds had thinned and lifted. Tess decided the clearing was some sort of old mountain omen: She would take the slow road, just take it fast. She picked up speed, racing along the farmland straightaway that swept south out of Springfield and then rose and fell when the Ozarks bucked up green. She rode high on the curves and felt the dips of the pavement low in her stomach as she headed into the oldest mountain range in the country, so old it had been worn down into nothing more than steep wooded hills with valleys just big enough for the clear-water creeks that rattled through them.

It had been a decade or more since she had ventured back. But now that she was here, she seemed to be shedding the intervening years as she would a winter coat: It was springtime. As if in welcome, the dogwoods were in bloom. She had seen them from the plane, like mist floating among all the filmy shades of May. And then she had noticed the pink of the redbuds, late enough this year to flower in unison with the dogwoods. It was a rare spring, the kind that had happened only once in her childhood. Her father had taken her out then for a Sunday drive. They had driven through these mountains by roller-coaster back roads, stopping along a spring that gurgled up out of some mossy rocks. They sat on the rocks as though they were velvet cushions, dangling their feet into water so cold it made their skin burn. The radio had played Bing Crosby that day and Dinah Shore. Pop whistled along until they drove out of range of that station and could only find country music. "Whiny crapola," her father had said, flicking it off. "Cryin'-in-your-beer music."

Her father had not believed in crying or whining or beer. She smiled at what he would have had to say if he could witness what had happened to her destination, to the little town where they had stopped that long-ago day for a vanilla Coke. Back then, Branson, Missouri, had a two-block main street and two mountain music shows, one in a barn and the other over the jail-house. From that beginning, Branson was now fast becoming the cryin'-in-your-beer capital of the country. According to the national reports Tess had seen, it was a boomtown. Longtime entertainers, people she remembered from 1970s television specials, were settling down in million-dollar music palaces: Andy Williams had come. The Osmond Brothers had a prime piece of real estate. Wayne Newton had a sign she'd heard you could read for sixteen miles. The old hillbilly-theme park where she had played now sprawled over whole miles. Cars crept in caravans of traffic along what had not so far past been a country road, their license plates reading like a Triple A road atlas of the states: Alabama, Alaska, Illinois, Montana, Tennessee, Wyoming. The hottest country stars journeyed up from Nashville in their plush buses, following the tourists. And journalists, such as herself, flew in from both coasts to report on it all—with a skeptical eyebrow cocked, of course. There was something too sincere about Branson for coastal types.

The sun was cracking through the clouds, throwing spotlights onto the farms that nestled in the valleys or perched on the hillsides. She looked at the cows grazing, the tractors turning up the wet fields, the early chicory blooming blue along the roadsides. Steam was rising off the highway. It felt good to be home, even if for just the space of one assignment. She eased up on the gas pedal so she could feel the car as it rode the contour of the land, as it found the shape of home.

Tess savored this, savored being behind the wheel, just rolling free. So often, she traveled by plane, zigzagging the country, setting down for a day here, a couple of hours there. Only last week, she had been out in Los Angeles, lounging by the Sunset Marquis pool, taking phone calls, and then nudging her rented Miata through traffic out to Malibu for an interview with a rough-hewn film star who was headlining studio movies. He was wildly famous for his John Wayne brand of upright machismo and of course he

4

would have fulfilled none of his fans' fantasies. Carefully observing his vegetarianism, which was strictly off the record, the man who wrangled beef on-screen ordered a Caesar salad hold the anchovies, and he and Tess talked as the orange globe of the sun dropped into the purple ocean and as the sky took on the bruised cast of night-time. In his low gravel growl, the star spoke of being misunderstood as a man and how he was reading books like *Iron John* "to sort through my issues." He was only surviving the "psychically grueling" days on location, he said, with English flower treatments. As if to illustrate, he kept getting out blue vials and squirting eyedroppers of liquid under his tongue. He showed Tess the impatiens tonic for soothing irritability and the cherry plum for coping with emotional emergencies. Afterward, she noticed he took a double dose of each when he got wrought up talking about a producer who nettled him. In fact, he squirted one extract or another until Tess lost count and he lost control and told her how *much* it would mean to him if he and Tess could stay in touch because this was Hollywood and no one *listened* here, *ever*. But she did, he said. He could tell she was *hearing* him. She didn't have the heart to answer him with the bald truth that of course she was being very well paid to hear him and that otherwise she doubted if she would be caught dead or otherwise listening to this American idol emoting into his essence of dandelion.

Anyway, she got enough scintillating insight to satisfy her editors at the celebrity magazine. At the end of the interview, Tess walked the actor to his Range Rover. He was in a hazy state, and she wasn't sure he should drive but felt too foolish suggesting that he might be intoxicated by the brandy in his flower remedies. He kissed her on the cheek, displaying that immediate intimacy that Hollywood had trademarked, and wheeled out of the parking lot. She sat in her rental for maybe five minutes before turning the key in the ignition and turning toward the hotel. She had driven with the wind in her hair on the way back and felt lonely and lost in the blue light of the rising moon. She didn't sleep well that night and had finally gone out to sit on her balcony overlooking the pool. She stayed for hours. White lights twinkled like stars in the courtyard trees, but when she looked up to the sky all she could see was the rusty haze of city lights trapped in smog.

The next day, the phone rang early. It was Logan, her editor, and she knew it even before she heard his voice. She knew it was 10:30 in New York and that he was having his bagel and reading six newspapers almost simultaneously. He was sitting there backlit by his window overlooking Times Square. He would be wearing something black from Barneys, his hair freshly cut in sharp angles. "How was Conrad?" he asked. "Delicious?"

"He nurses his inner child on flower juice. You'll love it." There, she had spun it already. She wanted to go back to sleep.

"Good girl," Logan said in the buoyant tone he only used when he was feeling good enough about himself as a Player to mimic the Triumvirate of editors who ran the show from corner offices. "I've got a reward for you."

Tired and a little burned-out, Tess groaned inwardly and then instantly rebuked herself. She did still find it unbelievable that stories now landed on her. In the early years of her career, she had lain in wait for each opportunity, reeling each in with care and guile. But this was her fourth trip in as many weeks. She'd had half a dozen cover stories already this year.

"Buck Campbell," Logan sang, as if he knew that name would dazzle her because it dazzled record producers and television execs and millions of fans. "Hottest thing in country music, darlin'! The Tom Hanks of Nashville. And you're just the gal to jump all over it."

The name shot adrenaline into her system. She felt her heart speed up as she untangled herself from the sheets, swept her wild hair out of her face.

No, she had said, No. She had said it for ten minutes as Logan practically choked on his bagel. Never had he come up against a refusal from her. "Have you had any chocolate yet?" he asked. "You ring up room service for some nice mocha, then we'll talk."

"Don't be condescending, Logan. I said no."

He began to wheedle, a whine humming along with his words. He tried stroking her ego, telling her only she could do it. Then he switched to trying to tantalize her by saying, "He's got a history that nobody's chiseled out of him." A note of panic rose above the whine, piercing, as it became clear that no appeal on professional grounds was going to work. And so he began to beg. "I already told them you would," he panted, meaning the Triumvirate, the men who held his life, his career, in their sway as each night they sat sipping whiskey, the sun setting in the wrap-around windows that made each of them look like the demigod in charge of this part of the sky. In the end, Logan pleaded in a long silence that boomed his desperation from coast to coast.

She hesitated, then asked where.

The next day, flying home to New York, she had looked down over the heartland, at the patchwork of farmland where she had grown up. It reminded her of the quilt she had slept under as a child. She could remember waking early and tracing with a fingernail the red-checked and blue-flowered and yellow-swirled patches that had once been her great-granny's apron or her granny's first dress. Tess had looked down from the plane, her heart faintly aching as she thought about Sunday mornings in the old Baptist church, the good people there who stroked her hair and sang with inelegant voices full of treasured conviction. She thought of swimming in the creek. She thought of the insects humming into the night and the cry of the whippoorwill. At last she closed her eyes only to see a vision of herself: She was flying over, high above her hometown and her people, trailing her wrenched-free roots like a wedding train.

Any other time, she would have refused the assignment that had brought her to this Missouri highway. She would have begged off, saying there just wasn't time before she went to England to visit the set of Hugh Grant's next film. She could have said that she didn't do country music stars, didn't know anything about that world, didn't care to. She could have worked herself free of being here.

But she had longed to go home. Tess had wanted to sit in dark theaters and hear plain-spun voices going back and forth in tones she had heard outside her bedroom as a child, in her classrooms, in the church. She wanted to feel not so alien. Strange, she thought, that she would come back to the Ozarks for comfort, when she had left in the first place because she never really could feel comfortable here. Yet it was true: She wanted to be here on this road more than she wanted to avoid seeing him. She still didn't know how she would face him, was ashamed that he was her excuse for coming away from the cities and getting home for a minute. She was discomfited that she hadn't said there were reasons she shouldn't interview this one celebrity, why she shouldn't get under his skin.

She hadn't said it, though. And when Logan had come into her office to continue pleading his case on Monday morning, he must have thought he'd found a way into her good graces by merely bringing her a brownie. It was an appeal to their friendship, which had started in the research department when they were all working fourteen-hour days and six-day weeks to make other people's writing accurate. He had brought her gourmet brownies then on deadline days, and she had sat in the smoking closet, choking, as he puffed nicotine and blew off steam about the indignities of being an editorial grunt. Tess and Logan had not climbed over each other to get where they were going. They had scrambled up the hill together, bound together by a tenacious boot-camp affection.

She would do the piece. For Logan partly. Because she was a professional. And maybe a little bit for some old part of herself that remembered those eyes. For whichever reason, for all

9

of them, she was here now, driving fast on this
road home.

CHAPTER TWO

Tess skirted Branson and headed south to the
lane that would take her to a lodge in the country-
side. Her magazine never quibbled about where
she stayed, no matter the cost. The Big Cedar
was the Ozarks' best, beyond the chasing lights
and the throbbing neon of Branson—and beyond
the immediate reach of Poe, who was staying
closer to the theater because he didn't drive and
liked to walk as part of a daily meditation. What
had he said? His guru, who had discovered the
gift of prophecy at age six, believed that when
you walk the blood pumps more forcefully from
your heart, ferrying your soul to your brain so that
the two become intertwined and begin working
together in a holistic symbiosis of the physical
and the spiritual. *Okay.*

So Poe was there in Branson, far away, forever
away. And she was turning down a long twisty
road that led to a place out of time, where she
could wake and hear the birds sing, where she
could go out in a boat at midnight or walk barefoot in new grass. As she wound down the lane
to the rustically but expensively appointed resort,
she notice several limousines outside the main
lodge. She nosed the car gingerly through a
stream that ran picturesquely over the road, and
a bellhop driving a golf cart greeted her, leading
the way to a cabin of her own, which was snuggled

in seclusion near the roots of a pine grove. The lake stretched out from its door. The ground was rusty with needles, and the air was sweet. Stepping from the car, she stretched into the sun like a morning glory.

The log cabin had a deep rock fireplace, ample plaid furniture, and stuffed game animals mounted decoratively on the walls. There was a deer bust over the mantel, and a bobcat stealthily stealing along a ledge over the kitchenette. There was even a squirrel on a branch that served as a bedpost. "I guess you don't have many animal-rights conventions here," she smirked as she swung her black leather duffel onto the reproduction Lone Star quilt covering the bed.

The bellhop grinned politely out of one side of his mouth and opened the balcony door to the soft breezes, wishing her a pleasant stay as he left with his tip. Tess took an apple out of her bag and sat outside. She leaned her head back into the sun and closed her eyes until the shimmer on the lake was just a dazzle of light. The warmth meant she was truly home, as close as she ever got anyway. Rarely anymore did she find a quiet moment and rarer still a place in the sun. When she was reporting in Hollywood, the light was just a glare, a spotlight for aerobics-sculpted beauties to stroll through on the arm of a white-haired mogul with leather hide and silk shirts. In New York, the sun cut through the buildings, throwing everything into contrast, slants of opposition. She hurried from one band of light to the shadows as she raced from her office on a thirty-second floor above a Broadway theater to a dark screening room to an interview in a clattering trattoria with Mondrian design. New York was all angles, and she slid along them from assignment to assignment. Sometimes after brunch on Sunday, she and a friend would wander through Central Park and pause in a swatch of sunshine to listen to the sizzling spice in a zydeco band or the pounding surf in a Jamaican rhythm group. New York came at her from all sides, and she didn't really feel any of it, couldn't. It spoke all different languages to her. She understood enough to succeed, but not enough to feel at home. She was intimate with the city the way she was with lovers from other continents: Communication was on solely a sensual level. That was the way Tess understood the city, by the way its traffic inarticulately roared beneath her windows, by the way its cappuccino tasted, and the way spring came to blanch the bare trees with flowers as they stood fast in their tiny squares of sidewalk earth.

But now here she was on the rocky ground of her mountain home. The pines, still glittering with drops of rain, gave up their perfume to the stirring air. Their aroma was as old as her memory, old as the cooling clasp of the lake that she had paddled around in an inner tube. She was home. The Ozarks settled over her like her great-granny's quilt.

Even as she exulted in this warmth, she endured a tugging awareness that she should be on the phone with New York. She knew she should be rushing her shower and shaking the wrinkles out of her dress. She needed to hurry if she wanted to eat before the concert. Instead, she ran a foot along the curve of her calf as the breeze toyed like a lover with the loose copper curls around her face. She knew the sun would prick up the freckles on her nose and that her green eyes would shine out from the sun-blush. She knew that she would look like a hometown girl. She would belong. This luxurious moment was smoothing the wrinkles out of her spirit, erasing New York from her face, melting Hollywood out of her soul. It was bringing her home to herself.

In New York, she had been transformed, not so much consciously as by Pavlovian response. "You're not from New York," someone would say to her when she paid cash in Bloomingdale's or gave up her seat on the M104 bus. Donald Trump had said it once when she called and asked a hard question in too soft a way. Slowly, she had evolved into one of those Manhattan hybrids—the canny out-of-towner who has grown up in a small place that never felt entirely like home and who learns to mimic the sophisticates, to do them one better, to ascend because of having already propelled herself out of a tight place. She had put on black tights and Lycra skirts. She had clipped the drawl out of her sentences. She had learned to stop drinking amaretto sours, which tasted better, and learned to start drinking wine, which *looked* better. Out in L.A., she had mastered the easy banter that said nothing if not that she knew her power and how to use it. She could pump power as easily as the free weights at the Vertical Club. But she was sick of power. She was powerless to give herself what she really wanted: moments like this, some stillness in her life, some peace. She wanted, for once, for her strength to serve her, to serve Tess Boone—not a magazine or an editor or her grand, grand career.

She brought the crook of her arm up to shade

13

her face. The sun and the light wind off the lake were conspiring to call up the scent of her skin, sweet as the smell of bread dough rising in her mother's kitchen. She remembered it from the days when she used to sunbathe in the backyard or roll in the leaves before her father burned them, or, later, from the moonlit nights when she would go out walking, her hand in his. There was something about being outside in the stirring air that made her more herself, made the most real things about her rise to the surface like air bubbles long caught on the underside of a submerged stone.

The phone began to ring.

CHAPTER THREE

The sunset was red in the lake as she wound her way into town. The traffic stretched like one long brake-light-spangled marquee, pulsing endlessly between the theaters. The reports she had seen on *60 Minutes,* read in *Entertainment Weekly,* had not prepared her. Branson had altered itself shockingly from the rustic little strip of "hillbilly" joints where common people had long gone to hear fiddlers play the "Orange Blossom Special." This looked to Tess like a wholesome Las Vegas, like a cleaned-up midwestern version of Broadway. The old Branson she held in her mind clashed with this blitz of neon. This new Branson even clashed with itself. She saw both Rolls-Royces and Chevy pickups. She saw teenagers in cutoffs and women in strapless gowns. Her granny would've declared it made hell look like

14

a lightning bug. But when Tess stepped from the car into the mid-May humidity, she caught the familiar smell of hickory-smoked barbecue. And smiled. For all its sprawl and glitz, she thought, Branson had not gone back on its raising.

She had showered and now felt fluid and free. She recalled a favorite expression of a former lover, a Frenchman. Tonight she understood what he had meant by it: She felt comfortable in her skin. Her limbs were smooth inside the floating gathers of her summer dress as she walked between the white columns of the Grand Palace and into its mulberry-colored rotunda. At the last minute, she hadn't put on her Eau de Givenchy perfume. Tonight it was enough to be only the self the Ozarks had coaxed out into the sun.

Immediately, Tess encountered the first obstacle to staying true to this reclaimed self: She spotted the man she knew had to be Poe. He stood out in the crowd of tourists. He was waiting by the door, a sparrow of a man who had been born in China, though it was impossible to tell by looking at him now how long ago. He seemed somehow ageless. He was mopping his earnest brow, having just hauled three bags of equipment through the moist air, freakishly hot for May. "This is like swimming in hot soup," he said after they had agreed that she was she and he was he. He picked up from their one phone conversation as though they had known each other for eons. "This is worse than New York in August," he grumbled. He was a gentle man but high-maintenance. He was going to expect a lot of her, in that Manhattan way that expected a team to ally their neuroses and help each other, which even

15

Tess had to admit was better than the alternative option, which was to throw friction sparks as you progressed through competition. She already knew she would have to disappoint his expectations.

"It's definitely not New York," she agreed as her gaze swept over the tourists who were clotting around the room, staring at the white baby grand that all the stars signed. There were tourists buying Branson ball caps in the gift shop, queuing up for GooGoo Clusters and Mountain Dew at the concession area. The colors of their clothing were simple and bright, striped and polka-dotted.

"These tourists," Poe said, gaping at the crowd as though he had come upon a herd of holstein cattle on Fifth Avenue. He was not so much unkind as astonished. She supposed that he had never orbited beyond American cities, had never seen real Americans. He had lived all his immigrant life in the province of New York, which could not accurately be described as belonging to the rest of the United States.

Still, Tess felt stung by his stranger eyes passing over these people, her people, then resentful that anything or anyone from New York should impinge upon her homecoming—even if she herself was slightly aghast at the way commercialism had blistered up in the Ozarks.

"Let's find the publicist," she said, and started toward the winding staircase that went up to the balcony. Poe trailed her, swiveling his eyes like a superpower beam that alighted on every blemish, every dear, singular Ozark eccentricity.

The publicist, Lisbeth, had been warmly efficient over the phone, and Tess had been so charmed to hear Missouri in her voice that she had relaxed her professional demeanor. So now Lisbeth, a woman who had fringe on her blouse and tassels on her white cowboy boots, greeted Tess by saying, "Welcome home." Tess felt a twinge. Maybe she shouldn't have revealed herself as being from the hills. She was working here. Especially on this story, she had to keep her professionalism up like a shield.

Poe said, "You didn't *tell* me." His tone was as genuinely surprised and hurt as though they had been friends for years and this had been something she had kept from him, betraying their intimacy. After all, he had divulged so much about his guru; while all the while she had willfully not told him the simple fact that she hailed from the Branson area.

Tess brushed both of them off by saying, "I hardly recognize it."

She suddenly longed to have her Manhattan anonymity armored around her. But she smiled politely as Lisbeth told her the arrangements had been made for the interview. She could go meet Buck Campbell backstage after his show. And then tomorrow arrange for a time to sit down together. "*Alone,*" Lisbeth said with emphasis. "*If* you can."

Tess arched an eyebrow in question. She knew Lisbeth was obliquely referring to Georgia Hill, Buck's wife and manager—his bodyguard, if you believed the gossip press. Tess was relieved she hadn't tossed off a mention that she knew Buck from way back.

"Not that you can blame her," Lisbeth whispered cryptically, a slyness creeping into her tone. "What he does for a pair of Wrangler's."

Tess felt color creeping hotly up her neck and

17

spreading. She wanted just to go take her seat and lose herself in the darkness of the theater, but Lisbeth pressed on: "He's gorgeous. And sweet. You can see how it could happen. Sweet men are ripe for the picking."

The floor seemed to tilt under Tess. "So where am I sitting?" she said in a tone that was more abrupt than she wished it had been. She berated herself for being rattled. But even as she did, things got worse. Tess saw a lithe young New Yorker coming toward her, curvaceous in her Lycra: Heather Trace.

"I heard you were the lucky one," Heather said, air-kissing Tess on the cheek. Tess hadn't seen or spoken to Heather since the young woman had abruptly left her magazine and gone over to the competition, *People*.

"Lucky?"

Lisbeth explained: "Buck Campbell's just doing the one interview before his world tour."

"You mean his wife's just *letting* him do one interview," Heather corrected, using an arch cattiness that made Tess cringe.

Again, Tess asked to be seated, brushing Heather and what she represented off. She didn't want to have to parry and thrust just now. She didn't want to invoke her New York skills. She just wanted to sit and listen to the voices that sounded like home.

Lisbeth guided them into the theater and showed Poe where he could cruise for photographs. She pointed out the stage door where they should all three meet afterward to go backstage for the first interview. Poe started off to ready himself only to turn back briefly to double-check the stage door with Tess. Finally, he swayed down front, adjusting his light meters and strobes.

Slipping into her seat, Tess floated on the small talk around her. Two women behind her were swapping tales about bargains at the outlet mall. She heard a couple gushing over hearing Loretta Lynn sing today and another couple arguing over whether Wayne Newton hadn't been a little *too* wild at last night's show. "He was talking geography," the husband scoffed, defending Newton's routine of reciting titillating place-names. "Those were *body* parts," the wife hissed back, scandal in her whisper.

Tess grinned discreetly into her hand. There was a lot of gray hair in the audience. Branson had become a magnet for the midwestern retirement set, situated as it was in the Bible Belt. It was the midwestern Palm Beach. Entertainers who got shoved off the airwaves by shock singers like Madonna and Michael Jackson had moved here and grown rich catering to the nostalgia of tourists who remembered a kinder, gentler America or at least one where hypocrisy reigned and most people kept up the pretense of decency. These tourists poured in by busloads and by RVs. And now the Grand Palace was trying to lure the younger families and teens by booking the hottest country stars, such as Garth Brooks, Alan Jackson, and Trisha Yearwood. Such as Buck Campbell.

Tess could see his fans scattered through the audience, congregated in the front rows. They wore sequins on their jean jackets. Their studded jeans were tight. Some wore red cowboy boots. And they seemed to like to draw their long blond hair into ponytails clasped by Native American sterling clips. But, most amazingly, many of them had on a black T-shirt that showed only Buck Campbell's backside—from the top of his white hat on down to his Wrangler's, then on down his long, long legs where one knee was cocked in sexy languor, finishing with the boots.

An electric anticipation was running like current through the aisles, and for the first time, Tess began to realize what he had become. It was years ago that she had been flicking through the music bins at Tower Records. His face had appeared to her then, a ghost on a plastic cover. She bought that first recording and walked up Columbus and then over to Riverside and up into the park. She watched the sun go down in a fuchsia smear over New Jersey. She had walked down Broadway with the CD throbbing at her rib cage, throbbing right through the leather of her backpack, throbbing like guilt itself. At home, she played it. She recognized something familiar hidden in among all the synthesized guitar, but it wasn't her Jamie. His name was Buck Campbell now. She played the CD only that once, never again. Later, she had watched the name Buck Campbell mount the *Billboard* charts. It had startled her the first time she saw his face on the cover of *Rolling Stone.* She had read the article, of course, and looked at the pictures of him at home with Georgia. The captions and the text were cagily crafted: Basically, he had been a young man in a slide, causing trouble, spending nights in jail, drinking. Georgia had rescued him one night after hearing him sing in a local bar and afterward had molded him to take the stage in her nightclub. She had poured herself into making sure that Nashville noticed this boy with his old-fashioned, break-your-heart style. As his star rose, they had quietly married, shocking Nashville and his fans. Tess could read between those lines. The reporter who had written them obviously thought Buck had something to hide. The rumors were that he maybe didn't prefer women. The rumors were that Georgia had something over him. Nobody wanted to believe that a man who wore his jeans like *that* could willingly marry a woman like Georgia. She was aged beyond her years with gauzy hair that looked too jet-black and too thin. She didn't have even faded beauty. She looked coarse, like a woman who had been worked hard byrough men all her life. Nobody could see it, the two of them together: Buck Campbell with Georgia Hill. But Tess could believe it. She knew Jamie.

That thought coursed blithely through her mind and brought her up short: Could she still say that she knew him? It had never occurred to her to question her tie to Jamie. But what of Buck Campbell? She and Jamie had belonged to each other. Maybe always would. But they had not spoken in well over a decade. She had thought of calling him once, flirted with the idea over one weekend, but why? What would it mean for either of them? She sometimes heard wisps of his songs on a passing radio and felt that she had just caught sight of an old friend. But did she know him anymore?

Tess had never learned to think of him as a star, in her magazine's sense of the word. Stars were her business. They didn't impress her. In fact, she had a well-informed disdain for celebrity and its trappings—the assistants who effaced themselves and did all the work, the hangers-on who coasted on the coattails and took fifteen percent, the press agents who spun a mundane human into a demigod. Tess could see through the facade of celebrity into the cold empty prison that it was. She could see that inside fame there was mostly just a lonely place where you sat and questioned your right to have all this attention. Tess knew that sometimes you started believing what everyone was saying and sometimes you just suffered your sense of self and waited for your fans to figure out what a fake you were. Sometimes, you got blinded by the spotlights until you couldn't see yourself clearly anymore. Whatever Buck Campbell was, whoever Jamie was now, he was a star. She could handle a star, she assured herself. Any star.

The curtain rose on the opening act, and the crowd began to collect a shared energy from that one source of light and sound, as though it were the sun. The band was raucously bright-sounding and was fronted by a Mandrell sister who flipped around in a short skirt and played a dozen instruments and glittered in the spotlight. And then Glen Campbell came on stage to play a bagpipe rendition of "Amazing Grace" as a laser-light Jesus wavered over his right shoulder. The audience rose to a standing ovation. Tess felt as though she had been transported to another realm, that this scene in Branson couldn't possibly share the same earth as the stage in New York where androgynous people danced in cat suits. When the curtain closed, everyone around Tess seemed to gather herself toward that moment when Buck would be there. Each knew he was already poised behind that royal pleat of velvet and soon he would be all there was in the room, in Branson, in the world. The crowd simmered in anticipation. As much time as Tess spent with celebrities, she was still surprised when she saw—or rather felt—them in the context of their fans. When she was doing the magazine's Springsteen cover, she had gone to a concert at the Garden. The surging responsiveness of the crowd had seemed to her like nothing so much as the kind of raucous worship she had witnessed in her small town when the tent revivals came, when the hellfire evangelists put a torch to the congregation's collective and highly flammable fears.

Suddenly, in a blinding wash of colored beams, Buck Campbell was there, casting a long shadow. The audience pounded around him like an ocean, and he stood in the lapping waves of their excitement and sang. Tess couldn't really hear him at first; she couldn't see him clearly. Around her, women were screaming and pushing toward the aisles with flowers in their hands and cameras slung over their shoulders. Tess watched them move toward him and stand gazing up, the yellow light spilling in reflection down on them. A grandmother in a pink polyester pantsuit strained upward with a red rose, and Buck stooped and took it from her. He blew her a kiss and waved the blossom. The crowd cheered. Women all but howled at this expression of what made him so dear. The grandmother walked back up the aisle holding her heart.

Tess looked at him. Three thousand pairs of eyes looked at him and saw a folksy cowboy, a country music star prized for the way he could strum your heart chords and make the hurt echo all through you, a star beloved for his down-home charm. "Common as Arkansas dirt" was the praise people gave him. He didn't just throw off an aura of sexuality. Women could look at him and see not only a fine-looking lover but a fine soul. Men couldn't begrudge him much because he was such a good ole boy, known to love water-skiing and dirt bikes and Bud.

But no one else saw him as Tess did. He was there only for her. His hair was still as straight and lank as it was when they used to wade in the creek down below her house. It stuck like gleaming straw out from underneath his hat, tawny as the fringe on his suede jacket. His grin was still a little lopsided. The whistle gap shone out between his teeth. His body was coiled steel, and his fingers were tender on the strings of his guitar. Sparks flew off the gold band on his wedding hand as he rode his long legs from one end of the stage to the other, singing into the oceanic roar of his fans. His boots were alligator. His faded Wrangler's were high and tight.

The lights squeezed into him until he seemed their very source. He was aglow, casting the audience into dark relief. The country-swing instruments in the bank hushed themselves down to where they could pick up his voice and carry it aloft. He began to sing into the darkness, all heartache. His eyes were closed. He sang a quiet rendition, so slow, of "I Fall to Pieces."

At last, Tess heard him. *You want me to act like we've never kissed; you want me to forget, pretend we've never met.* His voice lifted, tippled up her spine, raised the fine hairs along the sweep of her neck, her arms. It was just him and a quiet guitar doing a song she remembered. *And I've tried and I've tried but I haven't yet. You walk by and I fall to pieces.* The timbre of his voice contained him whole, as though he were caught in the amber of it. She had forgotten his voice, willed herself to forget from that first day years ago when she sat by a clear-running river and looked at the jewel-toned pebbles on the creekbed and chanted resolve to herself. *I fall to pieces each time someone speaks your name.* That voice called him up as everything he had once been to her: She felt the bristly stretch of his leg against hers, the whisk-ered brush of his lips as he whispered in her ear. She saw his eyes, his gray eyes. His voice vibrated through her nerves as though they were so many guitar chords: She became his instrument. *You tell me to find someone else to love, someone who'll love me too the way you used to do.* Everyone listened. But Tess heard. Jamie was here. His name in lights was Buck Campbell. But Jamie was here, singing all through her.

Tess was alone with him in the dark, alone with what she had denied to herself, to him. He was hers. She was his. Still. Always. As they had been when the night was black and the insects were the closest thing to a guitar, and he had held her against him and sung so that his song quivered through them and rose out of the stem of their embrace and went rushing after the stars. Back then, he sang only for her. He sang when they were driving at midnight along the blue back roads in his pickup or when they parked at the creek to be alone. He sang happy songs and sad. He sang what he couldn't say, and she alone heard him and held tighter to his waist even as one last note escaped off into the dark, and he bent to touch his lips to hers.

She felt as though a twin spotlight were fixed

25

on her and that he watched her as she watched him. He had to know she was there. But did he know she heard him? Could he know that she listened to him with a part of herself that had been gone since the last song he sang for her?

Sound is motion. It stirs the air, displaces space. Sound is invisible and yet has force enough to shatter glass, penetrate concrete walls, cause the earth to shudder. Tess now felt its power. The sound of Jamie's voice pierced to her heart. *You walk by and I fall to pieces.*

Before the curtain even fell, she hurtled for the door. She was vaguely aware of the crowd on its feet, swaying like waves to his song. She sensed a blunt twinge of obligation to stay and do the scheduled interview backstage. But couldn't.

She raced to her car and steered it out of Branson and down the winding roads that humped and fell, humped along the hillsides and fell into the hollows where the only music was the cicadas. She opened the windows and smelled spring heavy in the rushing wind that muffled what still echoed in the valleys of her memory.

There would be no interview.

CHAPTER FOUR

Remorse was bitter on her tongue, and Tess couldn't even eat the chocolate stashed in her backpack. She poured a glass of California chardonnay and rocked herself in a chair on the balcony, as her father had rocked her as a child. She was no longer comforted by the scent of pine.

She was tormented by it. She was tortured by everything she had only hours before sunk into as though into a warm bath. These insects, their peculiar violins, had once been the background music. The way the stars floated above the dark hills, the way the lake lapped silver against the shore, all these things had been woven into her old life here. Even the cry of the whippoorwill was a call to remember what she had done. Clearly, she could not take the comfort of this place without being forced to reexperience why she had left. Her mama had been right about one thing: Old sins throw long shadows.

Shivering in the warm night, she went inside and pulled the quilt off the bed and took it back to the balcony. The rhythm of the rocker on the redwood boards didn't soothe her, as Pop's rocker had calmed her when she was small and feverish in his arms. Instead, the sound became the fierce beat of her memory, rapping at her where she bruised easily, demanding her attention. All the things she had denied to herself for these years now returned to buffet her until she finally broke from the place far inside where Jamie's voice had penetrated. She felt a schism split up from the searing deep center of her chest, felt molten emotion work itself up until hot tears spilled down her cheeks.

This was grief. This was what she had never allowed herself. But sitting here, safe at last on home ground, she mourned what she had lost. She mourned Jamie's loss as a sculptor gouges away one sliver of stone at a time. Sliver by sliver, she chiseled until her grief stood monumental before her: his big rough hand holding hers as they walked in the dry pasture where the grasshoppers cleared a path for them. His skin, soft as chamois cloth, stretched taut over the stony muscles in his arms. The way, on that first date after his big football game, the way he had driven her all the distance to his friends' party without managing to say a single word, had only turned up Patsy Cline singing "Walking After Midnight." And how later that night after they had danced and roasted marshmallows by the bonfire he had led her down by the river and said the first words he ever said to her alone. He said, "I love you." She had hugged him then, reached so far up to encircle him and pull him close. She felt for the first time his hair against her cheek and lucidly thought even in the moment that it felt like a spring duckling's down; she had smelled the woody spice of his skin; she had been cinched into the safe lacing of his arms as they wrapped strong around her. Sensually, she had experienced him indelibly; engraving him on her memory in their first embrace. He had turned in a slow circle then, holding her up, her feet off the ground, and she had opened her eyes and watched the Milky Way, looking like it was revolving around just these two people who already seemed like one and would forever. Almost forever.

Almost. She now discovered that she had denied even to herself how much she had blamed her father for that *almost*. Although blame wasn't the right word. She had believed in Pop, put faith in the unerring rightness of his love and anything it would ask of her. That belief had been the reason she could go through with it. Pop was a good man, a decent man. His motives were unblemished. He had always only wanted what was best for his girl. And he had never been able to give much of the best to her. He was an adventurer trapped in a small town, a smaller life. He had worked hard for meager returns, dreaming of bigger things but never daring to go out and get them. He couldn't risk anything. There was his daughter to think of, his wife whom he loved, though she grew more and more impatient with him living so much in his head. Together, husband and wife turned out a good enough life. He came home gritty and spent from working a road crew; she tended several head of cattle and a garden so bountiful it fed the whole Baptist congregation for weeks at harvesttime. The family ate a good supper every night, and Pop could get in some reading before bedtime or walk along the water. Their little house sat on a bit of acreage that bordered the creek he had played in as a child. He had taught Tess to skip stones there and catch crawdaddies by letting them back into her hand. Still, for all the blessings, he had wished to travel, to live the adventures he had read about in the books he loved. In his bedroom, the walls were lined with planks that through the years he had filled with paperbacks and a few cherished hardcovers. He was determined that Tess would have more than books on a shelf, that she would have her chance.

His determination forced him against the hard wall of his wife. Tess used to lie curled under her quilt and hear her parents fighting even through the pillow she held over her ears. Mama would say that there was no reason under God's heaven that they shouldn't use Tessie's college fund to get the car they needed right now. Pop would say that there were 632 reasons right down the road in town. The six-hundred-some citizens of little Prosperity were every one of them a reason, a blinking red light warning away his daughter, their daughter. Didn't she want a better life for Tessie? Did she really want her to have to work a minimum-wage job all her life and wear herself out on babies she couldn't afford? This is no place for young people to make a go of it anymore, he said. Little farms are withering, can't make it anymore. Jobs don't exist. The mines are all closed. Didn't she want a better life for Tessie? But his wife insisted that she didn't see all that much wrong with this one—except he was so tight-fisted and fixed on this hare-brained idea. College, whoever heard of it. The family was here. Not a one of them had been to college; now why should Tess go?

Tess had only to look at her own mother to know why she couldn't stay. Disappointments had piled on Mama one after another until she was stooped under them, her hair an early gray. She had wanted a houseful of children, and had settled for one, a daughter. Her own body betrayed her, wouldn't bear more; though, if tested, her husband might have told her they couldn't do right by even one more child. Instead, Mama toiled long around the place, insisting that they keep the cattle so they would always have meat. She waitressed down at the cafe occasionally. It was no harder work than all the women in the town, than the women in every generation of her family, had done. And she might have been well satisfied if the relentless grind had been eased by equal pleasures. But she was excluded from her husband's enjoyment: Mama thought you shouldn't walk unless you had to get from one place to another, not as recreation. She didn't care to read more than a recipe or an article on losing weight that could be finished while she was sitting under the dryer at the beauty shop. As a girl, she had liked to dance, but her husband never had and wouldn't now that he had a growing daughter. And while she was devoted to her family, her husband couldn't stomach them. Her mother and sisters and first-cousins-once-removed were all prone to penny-ante feuding, and her husband flat out said his constitution couldn't take their bickering. So she went alone to see her folks. It was easier than dragging along her husband only to have him leave hurriedly, embarrassing her. The one comfort she kept was her faith. While her husband stayed home to read on Sunday mornings, she took her daughter down to the old Baptist church. Tess remembered Mama's voice as an imperfect sieve, but one that she strained every song through, and joyously. For a few bars of music once a week, Tess felt bound to her distant mother as they sang together of gathering at the river, of the lily of the valley.

But Tess knew she couldn't stay and find joy once a week in the Baptist hymnal. At night, in the circle of light cast by her bedside lamp, she wrote in little cloth-covered diaries. She charted her life, confessed her hopes, shared her fears. Sometimes she jotted quotations from books. One night, when she was only fourteen, she copied words that Charlotte Brontë had written in an altogether different century in an altogether different place, but it spoke for her: "Such a strong wish for wings. Such an urgent wish to see—to know—to learn." And truly her father's dreams for her had taken root early in the fertile

31

ground of her imagination. In fact, Tess couldn't distinguish her longing from his. Pop had read to her when he tucked her under the quilt, read Mark Twain escape stories and *Alice in Wonderland.* Sometimes he told true stories about things like the curse of King Tut, which made archaeologists die from nothing but a mosquito bite on the cheek, and amused her by revealing that Mozart had a foul mouth. He talked about a city of skyscrapers where anyone could make anything happen. His words raised whole worlds up in her imagination. Long after Pop had kissed her good night on the forehead, Tess saw the pyramids and the oceans and the cities built into the sky. She saw herself walking there. It became to her a realm so real that she hated to sleep and be banished from it.

As she grew, she read everything. Pop took her to the library on Saturday mornings, and she spent whole summers lying by the creek reading *Great Expectations* and *Jane Eyre.* She began to dream of someday writing herself. Teachers fueled her aspirations with praise. Her father's pride spurred her on, and she felt herself so keenly alien from the other kids that to spend a lifetime with them seemed a grim prospect. And so she lived in the imaginary kingdom her father had built at her bedside. She sowed her hopes there. But her aspirations wilted when she heard her parents' rancor grow and seep through the wall between her room and theirs. Times were getting meaner. Everyone was working more for less. And her mother could not forgive her husband for sacrificing so much for something you couldn't drive to church or set out on a supper plate, for something as intangible as a college education.

It was easier for Tess when Jamie came into her life. He was older, and something of a romantic figure, Arkansas style. When she moved up into the county high school, he was a year ahead of her and tight with the upperclassmen who jostled each other in the hallways, soaking up the attention and the envy of all the other kids. He played football heroically, and the whole county was intoxicated by the autumnal ritual of football. People flocked to the stadium and cheered as though it would make life better, because for one Friday night a week, it did. Blood roared with adrenaline. The people of Hickory County stood and cheered together, united by this one cause. Proud. Troubles lapsed before the glory of those boys charging one another on a pasture that the men of the county tamed with brush hogs and white paint and high-wattage lights.

Jamie immediately became like a magnet to Tess. She caught herself watching him, attracted not because he was a hero on the field, nor because he was the tallest kid in the school. Tess was drawn to him by the compelling force of her literary imagination: He was a woodscolt, which was the polite way of saying that he had no father to speak of. And his mother, who had waitressed at the Bend-in-the-Road bar, had left him when he was only six. He had ended up in the care of a retired preacher and his wife, the Reverend and Ma Calhoun, and had earned his keep by being entertaining and kind and grateful. And not only had he endured, but he had managed it without bitterness and without the meanness that the other boys sported. He was all the time hugging the English teacher, throwing a long arm over her shoulder and squeezing her so hard that she couldn't help but relinquish a smile that warmed the whole class. It had never hurt Jamie that he had those delicate eyes and a goofy smile that chipped through any hardness of heart. But he was not yet what you would call handsome.

Tess found him beautiful. Her eyes followed him as he shuttled end-to-end on the polished basketball court. She loved the way his arms swiveled out of his shoulders when he launched the ball toward the basket, the way the muscles in his legs stood out in relief when he leapt high in the air on a rebound. Her eyes trailed him down the football field when he barreled through the clashing colors and flashed into the end zone, carrying the ball. He was graceful in play and boisterous in victory. His hair after a game would spike out in all directions, and he would hug his teammates and beam. She remembered watching him walk up the hill to the showers. She liked the way he moved. Her attention to him advanced to the point where she could close her eyes over her homework assignment or at bedtime, and Jamie would stand up and walk through her fantasies with his singular gait. He began to move through all the worlds that lived in her imagination.

Sometimes, in school or when they were all at the Dairy Creme, he would graze her eyes with his. And then drop his gaze. He couldn't even look at her. He was notoriously shy with girls, only loosening up when he'd been down by Sugar Creek drinking Bud with his buddies—until homecoming, his senior year. The boys had trounced the rival county. Wild joy was erupting

34

all over the makeshift stadium—out by the goal-posts cheerleaders tossed pom-poms skyward; in the concession stand the Future Farmers of America club sprayed one another with Coca-Cola; on the forty-yard line, the football players hoisted one another into the air. The victory was rampaging through the bleachers and Tess and her cousin Lou stood leaping on the sidelines, clutching each other. The players surged around them, headed up the hill to the locker room. Jamie had caught her and leaned close to say, "Wait for me. I'll give you a ride."

There was to be a big bonfire in Jenkins's pasture. Everyone was going. Tess was going with Jamie. Her heart chanted that certainty: *With Jamie. With Jamie.* Out in the parking lot that circled the stadium like a beach, people climbed into pickups and drove reveling off into the dark, their cries reaching Tess long after they had disappeared around the curve. She was waiting at his pickup. He didn't come. The other players came and went until his truck was the only one left in the sloping expanse of the gravel lot. She shivered, hoping he hadn't meant someone else, hoping he would come. Her chant faltered, changed: *Will he come? Will he?* Finally, she saw him walking down the hill with his duffel flung over his shoulder. His hair was wet, and when he opened the door of his truck for her, the interior light showed the flush on his face. He didn't do anything more than smile furtively in her approximate direction as he climbed in and cranked the engine. He snapped a tape into the player, and Patsy Cline sang sorrow into the night as he drove the country miles to the party.

After that first date, after the kiss on the banks

35

of Sugar Creek, they became a constant: the two of them side by side in his old red pickup, his big yellow dog, Fescue, riding in the back. They were an unlikely pairing: Tess with her articulate ardor, her almost fierce intensity and hungry intellect; Jamie so strong-bodied and easygoing and silent. But they each knew the secret of the other. For all her urge to fly, Tess wanted to feel grounded and safe. She didn't want to feel so compelled to leave the nest. She wanted to feel protected. Jamie's arms around her came to symbolize a home where she could stay. Which, really, was what he wanted from her as well. He had told her about his mama, how she loved him yet had no choice but to leave because her boss was beating her. Even now, Jamie could only picture her one way—with "blood running down her face like tears." Tess could tell when he was thinking about his mama. He listened to a lot of Loretta Lynn then. That was his way—to reflect what he was feeling with music. He would play Hank Williams, or he would play Van Morrison. Once, after he saw a movie, he bought the sound track and played a Rachmaninoff theme that spoke all his longing and love. It was as though there were a place in each song that he could take her hand and lead her to, show her that it was a place inside him.

Early on, Tess took him home. She had known that Pop would not welcome Jamie. Pop had begrudged her every date she had ever had. He had begrudged them for her own good. He could only take her so far in getting out and up in the world. But he couldn't work against her heart. He knew this. He wasn't impressed by the way Jamie played football or basketball; Pop never even went to the games. He didn't care that Jamie did odd jobs after school so he could take Tess out to the drive-in over the state line, or for supper out at the truckstop café that served homemade rolls and turkey with dressing all year round. It didn't help matters that Jamie had no real family and that his football buddies were largely a rough bunch, prone to driving cars that rumbled rebelliously down the quiet streets of town. Worse, Pop saw what Tess loved: Jamie's gentleness. Maybe Pop even recognized something of himself in it. This was the danger, the only thing that would prevent her from finding her wings. Tess had always been a tough child, made of sinewy fiber. But he also knew that she had felt sorely her being so different from the other kids. If there was any way to get to Tess, it was by being gentle as her father and thinking the whole world spun off her.

Also, her mother approved. For a girl who had never felt her mother's approbation, it provided novel relief. Tess had unrelentingly been at odds with her mother. Tess would rather read than mend shirts or pull weeds or clear away the supper dishes. Tess never disguised the fact that she wanted to live in a bigger place, do bigger things. It had all rankled in her mother, who spoke bitter words at her. Once, when Tess had refused to sit by a boy in church because she said he smelled bad, her mother had slapped her hard across the face, spitting one word into her daughter's face: "Snob." It was a curse word. Her mother knew of nothing nastier.

But from the day Jamie started coming around, her mother's ever-present disapproval thawed. She smiled when he came to the door, and she stayed up past bedtime to sit at the kitchen table feeding him homemade gingersnaps and hot chocolate. He provoked her to laughter. Tess couldn't help being pleased and proud, especially because she noticed how the change in her mother softened Pop. Her father was drawn out of his bed, from behind his book to come and bask in the glow of a woman he had not seen but once or twice since their courtship and early marriage. She saw how her mother's happiness seemed to make Pop quell his fears, at least outwardly.

So with her parents' blessing, Tess stole hours to spend with Jamie. They walked up Stones Throw Mountain, where they could see their world laid out like a quilt. They floated in inner tubes along the rapids of the river and then stopped to loll in the deep slow-moving spots, his hand holding her foot so they wouldn't drift apart. They went to the drive-in, the colors swimming over their heads until they coalesced into moving pictures on the giant screen. Or they stayed down by the creek and put a blanket in the grass. They looked at the stars and named the brightest ones for each other. And afterward, at home, she slept each night in his old number 88 practice jersey. She hugged it around her when the voices in the other room rose and blew through her thin walls in the still hours. Only now everything harsh Tess heard was muffled, everything sharp was softened. She was living through Jamie. Sensation passed through his skin before hers.

One night Tess promised to be home to help Mama with sewing up some new curtains for the front room. The ladies from the new church were coming the next morning for a meeting, and Mama had finally scraped together the money for the material, a nice flower print. But she couldn't do it all herself in so short a time. Tess had French Club after school, and then she and Jamie had lingered down by the creek. Each loved the touch of the other, the nearness, and it was always hard to pull away and go home. So the sun was already down when she walked in and found her mother bent over the old 1940s machine. "Hey, Mama," Tess had said.

Her mother had not looked up as the sewing machine screamed through another seam. Tess had gone to stand closer, feeling the full scorching fury of her mother's turned back. She saw the bare windows, the piles of old curtains. "Can I help, Mama?" The needle marched over the new fabric.

Tess waited, strung up in the silence, then gave up. She turned to go and only then did her mother speak. "Where you goin' now?"

"To do my papers, I guess." Her applications for the university were due tomorrow, too. And she knew her father would be anxious to see her dot the final *i* and cross the last *t*.

"Get over here," her mother said, ladling out spleen with each word. "I could use your help. Do you think you can run this thing for once?"

Tess had never liked the sewing machine, even though she knew it had been the pride of her great-granny, who treasured it the last years of her life, used it after decades of sewing every stitch of clothing and bedding by hand. Tess just didn't like machinery and couldn't work up even a sentimental affection for this cast-iron Singer.

The bobbin always knotted up on her. The needle got away from her, and the fabric bunched. She sat now and fed the fabric through, going haltingly. Her mother stood nearby, pinning up the next hem. Tess faltered, then forged on.

"Your great-granny wouldn't hardly believe a girl of hers couldn't stitch up a simple seam," Mama said.

Just then, Tess ran over a fingertip with the needle. Blood spurted. Her mama reached to examine the damage to her finger, and Tess, even through her shame and pain, realized that her mother's worn-rough hands had not held one of her own in maybe a decade. Her eyes felt suddenly hot.

"If you had any work on these hands," Mama said, "they wouldn't be so quick to bleed." Her mother's voice was weighted with an exhaustion that didn't come merely from making curtains or planting potatoes. Tess looked at her own long fingers lying fragile in the callused cup of her mother's palm. Mama's fingertips had dirt ground into their own particular whorls and arches: Her secret self, her life story, was outlined there in the flesh, easy to read and full of hard truths. Tess was staring at their hands together when Pop came through the kitchen door. He stopped, surveyed the situation, and said he thought Tess had paperwork to finish. Tess looked up at her mother and answered him by saying she had promised to help. "I'll help your mama," he told her. "You go on."

So Tess had gone to her room. Before closing her door, she had heard her mother's voice, the words more sigh than speech: "It's just like anything else. If I want it done, I do it myself."

Tess read the questions on her application form through a glaze of tears.

She still hadn't told Jamie about the university. It was the only thing she kept from him as they gave each other everything. They walked on the hillside above the creek one sunset and came upon the old Robb place, a beautiful stone cottage. The widow Robb had died that spring, but her flowers—the lilacs, the irises, the forget-me-nots—were still blooming. Tess had always loved the place, and was touched by its emptiness. Jamie tried awkwardly to suggest that it might someday be theirs, but she skirted his meaning, said something that came out too harsh about not even being able to scrape up the money between them for a steak dinner at the Blue Top. Another night they were moving like two white moths around a fire down by their secret elbow in the creek. They were dancing. And when they sat down finally to stroke Fescue, Jamie began to sing. His voice was pure as the water from the spring behind her house, and it surprised her as much as the fresh water did on hot days when she dipped her hands full and washed her face. She had looked up at him and asked him if his mama taught him to sing like that. He had kissed her said, "No, I taught myself so I could sleep at night. After she was gone."

"You shouldn't have to sing your own lulla-bies," she told him, feeling tenderness well in her like tears.

He touched her face with the back of his hand, kissed her on the eyelids. "I wouldn't have to, Tessie, if you'd marry me."

Her eyes had flung open to his. He laughed as he caught her to him.

41

"I can't sing lullabies," she said, looking out into the darkness over his shoulder. "I can't carry a tune in a three-handled basket." She couldn't see any stars.

"You'd think of other ways to make me sleep," he whispered into her hair, before drawing her lips to his and drinking her in.

She laughed when he drew back to search an answer in her eyes. She pulled him closer and kissed him deeply enough to make him forget what he was asking and to make herself forget about those papers in the mail to the university.

Pop's generosity toward Tess and Jamie had ended one hot May day when he chanced upon them down at the swimming hole. They were twined around each other in the water, kissing. The pebbles crunched under his feet as he came to the creek's edge. Tess had looked up at him and gone hot as lava in the cold spring water. Disappointment had flared in Pop's eyes, but he had only squared his jaw and walked away with tight shoulders.

Soon afterward, he gave her his say, which she knew already. It was hard for him to come out with. She was sunbathing off the back porch, glistening with baby oil and thinking about the prom. Her little radio was tuned tinnily to a rock station. The singer, she remembered, had been Bob Seger, and the song one that she considered old because it had been out since she was a freshman.

She felt a shadow fall across her. It was Pop, who had been weeding all morning in the garden. The knees of his work clothes were dark with mud. "Tessie," he said, "don't get yourself in trouble."

She blushed. She was sure her blood had burned her redder than sunburn. "I won't, Pop," she mumbled, keeping her eyes closed. He didn't retreat.

"You'd be throwing away everything. It would be no kind of life." He waited for an answer.

"I know, Pop."

His voice was stretched thin with intensity: "A baby would ruin your life, shoot you down in flames."

She threw her arm across her eyes and from the shade of it, squinted up at Pop, who was only a dark silhouette in the brightness. "Pop," she pleaded, just wanting him to stop, leave her alone.

"It hurts me to say it," he persisted softly. "Jamie is a good kid. But he's not right for you. And you're not right for him. You'd only make each other miserable. He'll be content to stay right here in town and work hard, get his hands dirty. He'll be okay scraping by all his life. But you won't. I've ruined you for that and maybe I was wrong, putting ideas in your head, giving you books to read. But you're all but spoiled now for this life. You cry when you read *Jane Eyre*."

They were both quiet. She chewed her bottom lip and prayed that he would back off.

"Look at your mama and me," he said, and finally, "Do you understand?"

She had nodded. He put a hand on her hair, which she could feel resting heavily upon her long after he had turned back to his gardening.

Through the young weeks of summer as the lilacs bloomed and the dandelions went to fuzz, Pop never said another word, but his eyes cautioned her, gave constant counsel. He had already foretold that she and Jamie would have to part, shown her by his own example that love was something that didn't help you along, but held you down. All her life, Pop had never come right out and said that. But he had made it clear that her mother was what anchored him to earth, to his little plot of Arkansas soil, to the work that ground him down more each day. Pop had once told Tess that as a young man, still single, he had gone down to the university. He had stood outside the doors and looked up at its carved marble pediment in awe. Forcing himself, he had walked in and asked for the application forms. Back home in Prosperity, he filled them out. Then one night Tess's mama had come crying to him because his cousin had done her wrong, broken her heart. All along, Pop had been watching her, had harbored a longing for her. And now was his chance, but it would come only at the price of another. His insides gave under the force of his feeling for her; his ambition crumbled away in the face of her needing him, of her willingness to lay her burden on him. And so they had married. When Tess was filling out her journalism applications, he got his old papers out and showed them to her, yellow and crumbling around the edges. He had never even sent them in.

Sometimes in the dark of her bedroom, those papers rose up on the screen of her closed eyelids. She saw what they said.

CHAPTER FIVE

Tess came into the log cottage and crawled into the bed. The room, which had given such a cozy welcome, now felt oddly foreign. It ticked and gathered itself away darkly into far corners, left her utterly alone with herself. The bed seemed to tip. She held to it. Finally, she wept again, but harder this time. Sobs swept through her in seismic waves. She cracked open in raw sorrow as the past rushed out and took its place in her consciousness, came out into the light where she had not allowed it for all these years.

A night had come that far-off summer when everything had been decided. Coming in for supper, Pop had brought the letter confirming that full financial aid was after all available: Tess was going to the university. Her mother hadn't looked up from the stove, and when Tess had pressed for a reaction, Mama had turned and gone to stand in the last squares of sunlight on the front-room floor. "Aren't you happy for me?" Tess had asked again. "Don't you want me to have a chance?" Even as she spoke the words, she heard how they echoed with Pop's, how she had heard them time and again, used against Mama.

Her mother looked up at her, fury loud in her eyes. "A chance to be anything but *me*?"

The rest blurred. Tess remembered being burned first by shame then by pain and finally by an anger that blotted out her rational side.

Somewhere in there, Jamie had walked in. It must've been about the moment when Pop had reached to touch his wife and she had spit out at him: "I've never been good enough for you, either of you." And after that, Tess was ripping down the new curtains, trying to purge whatever it was that burned through her veins and throbbed behind her eyes.

Mama watched with arid intensity as Tess moved from one window to the next. Pop had rushed to stop her, and Tess sobbed in his embrace. When she looked up, Jamie was standing with one arm around her mother's shoulder.

"Happy birthday," Tess told him miserably.

They had taken his party down by Sugar Creek, just the two of them. Jamie had built a fire. Tess put candles on the cake she had baked for him, and he blew them out and teased her that it wasn't chocolate. "It's for you, not me," she had said glumly as he was reaching to hold her. He made her talk and then listened as she cried about how her mother didn't understand her, how she was completely like her father, nothing like her mother.

Jamie had started laughing: "You and your mama look at each other, and it's like lookin' in a mirror."

"I take after Pop's family," Tess had said, thinking of her red hair and her freckles, thinking of her mother's dark hair gone gray and her tawny Cherokee skin, thinking of the angry words that divided them.

Jamie went on: "I mean that she probably sees what could've been, and you see what might happen if you're not real careful." Tess looked at him, embarrassed by the way he saw into her, stunned that he could see what she could not. "You be fair to her, Tessie. Her life's not easy, but she's got a good heart."

Shame lowered her eyes. For certain, his was a better heart than hers. He had rescued Fescue from starving in a hayfield. He had not allowed himself bitterness. He had comforted Mama. And feeling all this, Tess could do nothing but change the subject and give him his gift, a second-hand guitar. He was surprised, didn't say anything but "Thank you, thank you," while running his fingers over the strings, tuning. He had learned to play when a traveling minister of music had stayed with the Calhouns during a revival. Jamie had taken to it naturally. And now as he wove his voice around the music he made, Tess began to feel calmer. She absorbed him, the way his hair was blond on his collar and the way the muscles moved in his neck as he sang. She watched his fingers move over the strings, gingerly but sure. He raised a house around them with his song, and she sat inside feeling more safe and loved than ever in her life. She remembered how he had once studied the palm of her hand, traced its lines with his fingertip. "This is the map of my whole world," he had told her. She had touched his face and found it wet with tears. "I never had a family before I had you," he said.

She thought of this as she sat in the yellow shelter of the fire, warmed herself in his song. He looked up at her from the guitar and smiled and that was when she couldn't help going to him, hushing him with a kiss. He put aside the instrument and drew her into his arms. She kissed his throat where the music had come from, moved

47

up along the sandpaper of his jawline, found the warm cushion of his lips again. His hands played over her, drawing music into the night, accompanied only by the whirring locusts, by the murmuring of Sugar Creek as it coursed by them and away.

Later, when they were still, Jamie had asked her when they could start waking up together under the same quilt. She had started crying again. He had sat holding her on his lap, stroking the hair away from her face as she mourned him already. That was when she had finally told him that she was going away. She could feel her words go through him like an electric shock. "Leaving me?" he had asked.

"I have to," she answered. It was all she could say.

"He's making you do this, isn't he?" he demanded.

She was silent. He shifted her weight off him and stalked into the blackness where the fire's light couldn't reach. Fescue followed him, turning to look once at her, pleading with his deep eyes.

She had walked home and sat up most of the night writing a letter, trying to explain. But of course she knew there was no explanation. Jamie would feel it to be a sin against him, and she guessed it was. She should have said something months ago. But he had been her one haven from the tug-of-war of home. When she had been with him, in his arms, the rest of the world had dimmed around them. She couldn't see into that surrounding obscurity. Her future, college, had receded into the dusky reaches that weren't now, weren't him. Other possibilities had just ceased to be when he was where she could touch him. She had only been greedy for the serenity of their time together down where the creek snuggled under the bluff, where they could be alone, outside time. And she loved him, she loved him, she loved him. Words were her strength, and they failed her. She finished the letter, though, and gave it to Pop in an envelope with Jamie's name written across it in blue ink. "Give it to him when he comes," she said, and left to drive south with Lou and some friends.

They went swimming at Buffalo River. She floated all day in the sun and watched the water as it held her up, deep and green and clear all the way to the bottom. She wished that life were like that, that you could see past the surface and down deep to the things that really mattered. Right now, it felt as though too many things really mattered, but she couldn't see past the glare on the surface of it all, the glare of everybody's fears and dreams and yearnings—Pop's, Jamie's, Mama's. Where was she in all of it? She couldn't see anymore. But she had chosen, and today she was knitting that decision into every fiber of her being, making it part of her, binding herself to it. She watched the fish flicker in the shallows. She jumped off a big rock and lost herself in the shock of the cold water that rushed along her body, chilling her clean. But all day, despite her resolve, she wondered if her letter was in Jamie's hands. She saw his fingers, his skin rough from the field work, the black moon on his thumbnail where he had caught it in a loose hook on the baler. She saw his hands holding the letter. She could only see his hands. She could not see his face.

That night, instead of going home for supper, she had gone to a drive-in movie with her girl-friends. They had stopped by Pizza Villa. "To frat guys," her friends said, toasting Tess with their Pepsis. They were all staying home. Two were getting married that summer. Lou was finishing beauty school. They were excited about their own lives and sort of bewildered about hers. But they tried anyway to give her a festive send-off. They were curious to watch her, see what she could do. Their mamas were skeptical, had always thought the Boone girl put on airs.

Tess bit into her pepperoni slice and her mouth closed around a sliver of metal. She recoiled and inspected the triangle of dough and sauce. Somehow a piece of aluminum can had been loaded onto the pizza, buried under the cheese. It didn't cut her, but she couldn't forget the taste of metal on her tongue. She couldn't eat another bite.

Jamie came looking for her. His friends told her later that he had driven the hour to the lake and checked all their usual spots. He backtracked south and drove past Prosperity, on to Buffalo River, but must have just missed them. He hadn't thought of the drive-in. He didn't find her until the next morning. Pop went out to get the morning paper and discovered Jamie sitting on the front porch.

"Tessie," Pop said, standing in the doorway to her bedroom. "You better come talk to Jamie."

She had pulled her chenille robe around her and gone barefoot to stand before him on the gray-painted boards of the porch.

"Look me in the eye, and tell me you mean it," he said. He was shaking. And he couldn't

50

keep it out of his voice. He stood in silence, his demand clearly one he wasn't going to be refused.

Finally, she brought her eyes up to meet the intensity of his gaze. His gray eyes were wet.

She searched but couldn't find the words. And it seemed like forever before he just turned and walked down the steps and away.

Pop caught her in his arms as soon as the screen door closed behind her. He held her, rocked her a little in the morning light until his wife said tersely and fed up with it all, "Come on now and eat."

She had gone away, gone through with it. Pop had driven her down to the college and dropped her off. For the first five hours she was there, she had lain on the mattress on the floor, her only furniture, and stared at the way the light was dying across this ceiling that she had never set eyes on before in her life and that was now what she was going to wake up to for the years she could foresee. She had never been away from home, and home was now behind the wheel, driving farther and farther away. Pop was leaving her to this. Abandoned, she didn't get up until she knew Pop would be pulling back into the driveway in Prosperity—until it was irrevocable. She would be staying. Then she had dived into college as though she were leaping off the knotted rope swing into Sugar Creek. It was cold and jolting. It chilled her through. It braced her against the sore part of her insides that gradually grew smaller and more still. She made the grades. She sent home clippings from the newspaper every time a story appeared under her byline. She even called long-distance her junior year when she won the coveted internship in New York City. Pop had offered her money, but she had said no, she would be earning more than she had ever seen in her life. She had gone. She had forced herself down into the subway at Astor Place and up into the tops of the skyscrapers at Rockefeller Center. She ate bagels, which she loved loaded with mounds of cream cheese; she sipped wine, which tasted as bad as medicine; and she had vowed to come back. And stay.

She had heard from people at home that Jamie had taken off, hadn't stayed more than a month after she had gone to the university. He'd been drinking a lot, had caused the Calhouns trouble for the first time since he had come to live with them. He'd driven through a wall of their barn and lost his job or just quit it. Nobody seemed to know. Anyway, he was gone. Nobody admitted to knowing where.

Pop came up for her graduation. She was surprised that Mama hadn't accompanied him for this at least, but he had brushed aside her questions until after the ceremony. At lunch, he finally confessed that her mama had left him. For some time, she had been going for Sunday worship and Wednesday Bible studies to a church over the state line, a kind of rogue fundamentalist congregation that called itself the Second Coming Church. They were led by a preacher named Brother Jack Daniels, and Pop had written in his letters, spoofingly, that all his disciples seemed drunk off him all right. Pop had never been one to stand between his wife and her religion. It meant too much to her. Mark Twain had talked *his* wife out of her faith, Pop once told Tess, and then she had no comfort when her child died. And so Pop had held himself back and simply watched as Mama lost herself in this, watched until the day she came home and quoted the Bible saying, "Thou shalt not be unequally yoked." She explained that since she was born again, and he was a heathen who sat home and read fiction books on the Sabbath, they were unequal. She hadn't said she was going off with an elder. Pop had found that part out later, when people from Prosperity started seeing her with a widower from the Second Coming flock.

Tess had reeled. Her mama? Tess had insisted on going back home with Pop. She would stay, she promised, so the house wouldn't be so quiet around him. He let her stay two weeks, until he knew she would lose her new job if she didn't go on to New York, where the people at the magazine had been kind enough to wait even this long. He forced her. He said he would be okay. She saw him once more at Christmas. He had taken to sitting on the porch even in the cold, and on her last night home, he said, "I was wrong to do what I did."

She thought he might be talking about not eating all his ham at supper or about her mama leaving or about anything. All the long week of carols and fudge and twinkling lights, Pop had been blaming himself for the whole world's troubles.

"You couldn't have known she would leave," Tess said, guessing that he meant his wife's taking off.

"I was wrong to you," he said. "And to Jamie."

"Pop," she began.

He held up his hand to halt her protest. "I was," he said sternly, his voice so heavy with tragedy that it seemed to creak with the weight. "He'll go to his grave loving you."

CHAPTER SIX

Ringing pummeled her until she woke and dragged herself from the catfish depths of sleep. Her veins ran with lead. She felt poisoned. Leaving the phone unanswered, she untangled herself from the sheets and looked in the mirror, splashed water on her red eyes. The phone stopped.

Tess found her favorite French-roast cinnamon coffee in her backpack and started a pot. The phone rang again.

She had to think. How was she going to extract herself from this? She could not, after all, go through with the interview. But what was she going to say? The phone stopped ringing.

She swirled milk into her coffee and stood on the porch. The ringing began again and stopped again. Poe? Lisbeth? Logan, by now? Why hadn't she shown up backstage?

The morning light was warm on her bare legs. It seemed to stroke her with tender hands. She let it have its way with her as the caffeine hit her heart and began to pump some spirit through her. It had been yesterday's lunch she had last eaten a meal, and so she ordered blueberry pancakes with warm maple syrup: comfort food. When the phone rang again, she was relaxed enough to answer it reflexively.

Poe said, "Tess?"

"Yes."

"Is everything all right with you? I mean, last night was very strange. Where did you go? And I've been calling already for an hour this morning." He hesitated between every question, hoping that she would jump in and spare him from asking more; prying wasn't in his nature.

"Sorry," she said finally. "I got upset suddenly. I had to leave."

"Your stomach?" he asked. "My guru knows the herbs to settle—"

"Never mind," she said.

"It is unfortunate to upset the balance of things, the appointed course." He paused, and added frankly: "I mean, I was in a tight place. The wife was very angry, very angry."

"Just because I wasn't there?"

"Of course," he said, surprised that she should be surprised. "We had a commitment, you know. And these people, they're not used to being jilted. They prefer the appointed course."

"Have you got your cover shoot set up?" she asked.

"Tentatively. But I really don't want to go forward until you have a chance to spend some time with Buck, get a feel for him, a sense of his soul," Poe said. His tone sounded like there was a strain of hysteria that wanted to rise to the surface. He was squelching it.

"Look," she snapped. "You're gonna have to go ahead without me. Just point and shoot." She immediately felt shamed by her sharpness.

"It's not the way I work," he said, the hysteria whining audibly. "It is a sharing process. Your vision completes mine. I work with synchronicity." He didn't deserve this, she knew.

Professionalism had been something she mastered early on because it was so like her father's code of ethics. There were rules, and you abided by them. She was breaking those rules now, had been breaking them from the moment she accepted the assignment from her unwitting editor.

"What time are you talking about?"

"Three."

"I'll get back to you."

She wasn't any less confused, still far from persuaded that she should go through with this. But she needed time to extricate herself in a way that would do the least damage.

She threw on her bathing suit, grabbed a towel, and headed down to the crescent of sand just beyond her door. The water nipped at her ankles, bidding her to let it take her burden. She progressed slowly. It still had the chill of winter in it. She waded out, tucked her legs, and, true to its promise, it carried her, just as the river had on the day she had given Jamie that awful letter, the day she had been too cowardly to say that he was too much for her.

The sky was blue, and a dove cooed in its mournful voice. Birds warbled and burst out with snatches of song. Tess began to swim with strong strokes, pulling herself far out from shore. She felt the muscles in her legs working together, the long muscles in the back of her arms. This was real. This was no StairMaster exercise. Her body remembered how to do this, remembered this very lake where she had first learned these strokes when Pop had brought the family camping. She went under and pulled hard so that the water ran over her body like silk veils. As a child, she had been afraid of swimming underwater until she had remembered something she had heard from the Baptist pulpit, that God had his eye on the sparrow and always on each of us. So she had begun to make herself arc downward, sure that underwater only God could see her. She had felt holy there, in the depths. *Mama doesn't know where I am,* she would think. *Pop can't find me. I am invisible except to God.* Far out, Tess surfaced and treaded water in the shining expanse of the lake. In the distance, she saw sailboats. A party barge cruised by playing a Nanci Griffith song that carried clearly over the water. She felt suspended, but finally turned and swam back to shore, staying underwater, keeping in God's sight.

Other eyes were on her when she bloomed out of the lake, flushed. She sensed it, could almost feel it like sunshine falling across her. But the daylight seemed blindingly bright after the shadows underwater. Tess squinted into the shade of the pine grove, saw nothing.

She waded onto the bank, oddly conscious of the water that at first gleamed along her body, a glistening second skin that finally parted into rivulets and ran to the sand around her feet. She reached for her towel and swabbed herself off as she walked back to the cottage.

There was an envelope propped against the door. Her name was printed on it in black ink. With a jolt, she recognized the hand that had written it.

Inside, he had scrawled one word: *Stay.*

CHAPTER SEVEN

Tess was caught. She couldn't leave without seeing him again, even if it meant just sitting across from him in an interview, even if it meant having to see him with his wife. He had asked. Or challenged. She wouldn't deny him, couldn't deny herself.

She walked slowly to the place where Poe had arranged to shoot the cover picture. The usually docile photographer was in as foul a mood as permitted by his guru. Georgia had refused to bring Buck into town for the photo session, and Poe had hoped that Tess would come to Branson to fetch him back out to Big Cedar. But by the time she called him after her swim, there hadn't been time, and he had been forced to hire a ride. He was still dragging his heavy equipment out of a van and trying to set it up on the banks of the lake.

"I need time," Poe groused meekly. "I'm off balance. I need to reconnect with my peace." There was a glaze of perspiration on his crinkled brow. "My creative eye is clouded by stress. And now there is no time." Tess could see his hands shaking. He wasn't counterfeiting a delicate constitution. Her heart went out to him even as his plight struck her as somewhat comical.

Suppressing her amusement, she tried to pacify him. She made him go walk along the shore in the shade of the hardwoods while she pulled his equipment under an ancient oak and tested her tape recorder's batteries. When she looked up, Poe was scurrying up the hill. She checked her watch and saw why. She was late. She took a deep breath.

"You go," Poe said. "You go. I will be ready when you come back." She left him in a blue tornado of activity, speaking low to himself. She couldn't tell if he was muttering in Chinese or chanting some spiritual mantra from his guru.

Steeling herself, Tess strode quickly in the direction of the main lodge. Almost immediately, she saw Heather Trace approaching. It wasn't the worst thing to have snubbed Heather a little last night. After all, she was a competitor now. But she was also only twenty-five and handicapped by naivete. Plus, Tess had always liked her—even after Heather had gotten her navel pierced and shown it off to the suspendered editors at the office.

"He's staying here, isn't he?" Heather opened.

"Who?" Tess feigned. She kept walking.

"Buck Campbell."

"Aren't you the competition?" Tess teased her.

Heather seemed taken aback, a little hurt. Tess said meaningfully: "I would help you, Heather, but I'm late for my interview."

Heather stopped, her hands fisted on her hips. "You don't think I can do it, do you?"

Tess exhaled impatiently, annoyed anew by Heather's penchant for reading something into everything. Tess wanted to say that she was sure Heather could and would do anything she wanted. She wanted to say that she had seen Heather take the head start of an Ivy League education and then stretch it by taking every shortcut ever created for beautiful people.

59

Instead, she said, "You're like a dang bull going through cobwebs."

"What?" Heather croaked.

"That's Ozark for you'll do whatever you mean to do."

Tess walked on, looking up at the lodge. Lisbeth had told her the Campbell entourage was staying in the penthouse suite. She could see the windows up under the arching eaves of the grand old building and wondered if they were watching her, if he was. She wondered if Georgia even knew there was ample reason to watch her. Tess didn't know what to expect from Georgia, or from Jamie for that matter.

The elevator was slow, and she pushed the button several times, although she had lived in New York long enough to know that you couldn't hurry an elevator. She just hated being late, was never late to an interview. It meant a loss of control, a sliver loss that could be wedged into an abyss if the personalities didn't slide alongside one another, click together naturally. And this was the absolute worst time to risk opening an abyss. She needed things to fall into place. She needed to coast through this by habit. Any surprises and she feared her wits might forsake her.

She rang the bell, inhaled deeply. Footfalls rang across hardwood floors, and a petite woman with a face that somehow coordinated with her buckskin leather skirt opened the door on a suite filled with stuffed game and polished walnut and woven patterns. The woman held out her hand. "Georgia Hill," she said as Tess took her hand, trying to apply the proper amount of pressure as it flashed through her mind: *This is her flesh I'm touching, the hand of the woman who lies every night in his bed.* Tess had seen her picture in magazines, but she was nonetheless shocked. In person, Georgia's flesh looked as though it had been applied haphazardly, whole handfuls bunched in the wrong place. Her face was deeply lined from too much sun or drink or trouble. Her mouth was tight and grim. "You must be Tess," Georgia said.

Tess nodded as Jamie advanced toward her, high in the boots that echoed under the soaring ceiling. He smiled and held out his hand. "Buck Campbell," he said. "Thought you might stand me up twice." Grinning, he looked her straight in the eye and watched for the double meaning to hit her.

It struck home like a slap, though she was certain he was only teasing her. Wasn't he? She flinched inwardly, tried to hold her surprise captive, tried not to let it show on her face. "Tess Boone," she said.

"Feeling better?" Georgia asked. Her tone was not unkind.

"Much," Tess answered. "Sorry for the trouble."

"No trouble for us," Georgia assured her. "You'll just have less time with Buck."

Ah-ha, Tess thought, here was a woman who could turn the screw of control.

Georgia went on to inform Tess that as Buck's manager she needed to do some business with California before the concert tonight. And as they were behind schedule (meaning, due to Tess's late arrival), they needed to get started with the interview so she could get back to the phone.

Tess swallowed and said, "Of course."

Georgia directed her to a cluster of deep, forest-green chairs arranged near French doors that looked out over the lake, then offered lemonade. "I'd love some," Tess said amiably, "since we're having August in May. This is how the greenhouse effect starts, right?"

Tess had already decided not to bypass idle chat; in this instance, as in others, it was a way of spending time to buy greater openness later in the interview. And so the three of them small-talked about Branson and how it was threatening Nashville's traditional role as the country music capital. Buck confided that he liked Branson better because down in Tennessee you couldn't go bass fishing with Mel Tillis and Shoji Tabuchi. As he spoke, Tess tried to concentrate on her note-taking, on whether or not the tape recorder's little wheels were turning. But she couldn't help wondering if his affinity for Branson had anything to do with its proximity to home, couldn't help wondering what home even meant to him anymore. She looked up at him casually, as she would make eye contact with anyone she was interviewing. His eyes locked onto hers, shocking as a live wire. She wrenched herself free and tried to concentrate as Georgia asserted a wish for a whole week to make the rounds of Andy Williams and Johnny Cash and Loretta Lynn, for "old time's sake," she said, as if to imply that if indeed Branson was capturing a segment of the market, it was only the gray-haired segment and not the young vital tight-fitting-jeans part that Nashville did best.

For Tess, it was slippery going. She wished to be safely obscured behind tinted glass, to be invisible. She hewed to a stream of chatty questions, seemingly unable to pick up speed and steer the interview to anything more direct. She rationalized to herself that she was only trying to make the other woman feel as though this particular journalist were someone to trust, someone to whom she could confide. But deep down, Tess knew that her professional side had been lost to the girl who loved this beautiful man sitting across a bearskin rug from her. And who was he, this moment? Could she trust him? Interviewing meant getting the subjects to cast aside their masquerade, but she, more than either Georgia or Buck, was having the most trouble keeping her mask in place. Usually, Tess stripped away a star's costume by sharing something of herself; then all they had to do was reciprocate. They didn't have to get naked alone.

Now she didn't have the luxury of sharing herself, and Georgia Hill was iron-clad. Try as she might, Tess couldn't get the woman to even lean back and relax against the love seat where she sat, her shoulder brushing Buck's. As his wife and business partner, she must have been through this hundreds of times, but Tess guessed that being interviewed was too passive a form to suit Georgia's skills. She seemed like the kind of person who could marshal troops, conduct a symphony, choreograph a Broadway musical.

And so the interview meandered. Georgia did not touch her husband. He did not touch her, but instead persisted in reclining against the love seat, steadily watching Tess, beckoning her eyes to his. For her, it was taking too much energy just to fight his gaze.

Summoning some reserve of professionalism, Tess tried finally to move past the get-acquainted preliminaries, to move into the fast lane, to get to the story. She asked how they had met, bracing herself for an answer she truly didn't care to hear.

"When I found him," Georgia said, "he was a stray pup, just a little stray pup." Her voice seemed to fall into a mode of recitation. "And I took him in and cleaned him up." Evasive, Tess thought. This was slick and calculated and well rehearsed. Tess had read it all before in the press clips Logan had FedExed from the magazine's library.

"True enough," Buck said. "She saved my life."

"From what?"

Georgia answered, rapid-fire: "Fighting and drinking and going around with the wrong women."

Tess scribbled furiously in her reporter's notebook. She scribbled not words, just the raw energy of her emotions as they spilled out in jagged scrawls of ink.

"She put that to a stop right quick," Buck said. His voice was different now, practiced.

The back-and-forth of the banter made Tess sure that it was some sort of routine they had worked up for just such occasions as this one. Tess hardly recognized Jamie in the man sitting with one booted ankle resting on his other knee. This was his Buck Campbell persona. He elongated his vowels, draped out his sentences. He stretched a full southern drawl out of the Ozark accent that on its own only lingered gently on unexpected syllables.

One sentence—*I hate this, I hate this*—kept looping through her mind like the running marquee at the Grand Palace. She wrote it in her notebook, among the notes. *I hate this.*

Tess asked Buck what got him up on the stage and performing. Georgia answered that it was because of how much he admired Hank Williams. Tess asked Buck when he first knew he wanted to be a country singer. Georgia answered that it was when he used to get up on Sunday mornings and sing hymns in front of the whole congregation. "Broke everyone's heart," she said.

P-leasssse, Tess thought, recognizing it for the lie it was. *He sang for me.* And then she couldn't help herself, she said, "I never knew that." It sounded like a challenge because it was. She tried to dull it by adding that she had never read it in any press account, but she had let it get personal. She knew it. Buck grinned; he probably knew. But did his wife?

Georgia bristled. "I'm telling you *now,*" she said caustically. "That is the point of an interview." And then she huffed imperially, "You can't believe everything you read anyway."

Something roared up fiercely in Tess, in response to the evasion, in response to the agony of being forced to play out this charade. "What *can* you believe?" she asked, fixing the other woman with a gaze that communicated that, yes, she did mean what Georgia feared she meant. What was she doing married to this man who had made show business history in a few short years, this man adored by millions? How had she accomplished it?

Georgia stared back. Peripherally, Tess noticed that Buck looked at his hands.

The journalist in her pressed on—fueled, though, by the old passion lurking in her blood:

"You know the rumors. You read the press. Tell me something we don't all know, something I haven't read in *People*. Clear it up."

Georgia nailed her with a ferocious look. And Tess welcomed it almost. It was the same feeling she had some days when she got on the subway hoping someone would shove her so she could have the marvelous release of shoving back. Now, in this moment, she was angry, unreasonably angry. She couldn't fully account for the bile that seemed to be pumping from her heart to every limb, into every word she spoke. Was she angry at this woman for being married to her Jamie? Was she incensed by his glib greeting, by his inscrutability? She glared straight into Georgia's eyes, waiting for her answer.

A door opened at the far end of the room. An assistant came out and apologetically told Georgia that the phone call she had been waiting for had come. Georgia got up from the love seat, crossed the room in almost a march, and closed the door behind her, leaving Tess alone with Buck Campbell.

Tess stared hard at her notebook. He stared at her, bright as oncoming headlights.

"Any hard questions you wanna ask me?" he said, his tone even, giving her no hints.

"Yeah," she said. "How long does it take them to get the spotlight fixed just right on your butt?"

He laughed, but she didn't look up, just kept running her pen over the lines of her notebook. And then there was only silence, and his eyes on her. She ended the pretense of going over her notes and said, "Stop staring."

Jamie spoke: "I've gotta get a good look at you. I know how fast you disappear." She still couldn't

66

read his voice, and she was losing control of herself. Her eyes came up to meet his, and her emotions followed. She felt the hot remorse and shame and old longing well into her eyes.

She saw how it surprised him: The acknowledgement of her tears crossed his face like the shadow of a cloud. He leaned forward as if to take her hand. But before Tess had even sensed anything outside the two of them and this moment, he straightened up, backing away. And just then Georgia came back in. Tess swabbed the corners of her eyes discreetly, but Georgia wasn't the kind to miss anything. Her tone was brusque, if a bit bewildered, when she said, "Let's get this over with."

"Has success changed you?" Tess asked, and watched for Buck to register the layers of meaning. His eyes fastened on hers as though they were still alone in the room. But Georgia answered: "He's not the same guy. He's tougher now. He won't let people walk all over him."

"No," Buck said to his wife. "You're the tough one. I don't have to be."

"When I found him," Georgia continued, "he was playing in sawdust bars and making nothing more than his bar tab. He was living off the peanuts and pretzels. He was everybody's favorite. The women adored him, and so he'd end up in fights with drunken boyfriends. His voice was getting totally ignored. Nobody was *listening* to him." When she emphasized the listening, she brought her hand not to her ear, but to her heart.

"And then I heard him," Georgia said. "And I'm sitting in that bar, where a client had taken me slumming, and I'm looking around the room and I'm thinking, *Am I the only one who hears this guy, who hears that instrument he has for a voice?*

"I was. I swear nobody heard him the way I did. Maybe I just heard him the way he could be." A look of triumph came over her. "But everybody's listening now."

Georgia reeled off the platinum records that hung in their Montana ranch home, the long string of number-one hits. She talked about his being named country star of the year three years running and about his crossover appeal. She ticked off his awards, counting on fingers with both hands. She talked about the television specials, the magazine covers.

"Georgia's my success," Buck said, trying to deflect her away from singing his praise.

Disarmed, Georgia laughed lightly and patted the denim along his upper leg. She smiled over at him. *She loves him*, Tess thought. And Buck Campbell smiled back at his wife. Afterward, Tess could not look at him.

Checking her wristwatch, Georgia said, "I'm behind." She stood to signal that the interview was over, that it was time Buck moved on to his photo session. "You've got him for two hours," she informed Tess coolly. "No more."

"Come right back," she instructed her husband. "You've got papers to sign before we put you on stage."

"Yes'm," he said, teasing her as she brushed the suede knapp of his fawn-colored fringed jacket as though he were a schoolboy.

"Take your hat," she reminded him as she turned away. He followed her with his eyes as she crossed the room and closed the bedroom door behind her. Tess cast off for the door, not waiting for him. She rushed to the stairs, winding down from landing to landing. He caught up with her. He called her name, but when she didn't answer, he followed her silently to the lobby, where other people looked up and noted their descent. Tess heard the first whisper of recognition, heard it strike like a match and spread like a brushfire.

Poe was on the porch to greet them, and a handful of people bobbed in the wake Buck Campbell made walking across the lawn. Heather matched his stride and tucked a business card into his hand; her photographer aimed and shot. Buck just kept moving until a little girl darted up, and then he knelt, signed his name, and chucked her under the chin so that her parents beamed proudly. Afterward, he waved people back, told them he was working even if it looked like he was just loafing. His fans stayed politely back.

"See, nice shade," Poe announced to Buck with a flourish of one graceful hand as they approached the photographic studio set up on the lawn. "Not too hot."

"I see that, buddy," Buck said, appreciatively pounding the little photographer on the back. Tess saw Poe's knees buckle, and she had to squelch a smile as he regained his bearing enough to arrange Buck with the lake behind him and the bluff beyond.

The singer had his big trademark Stetson on. "How do I look?" he said, pulling at the lapels of his jacket to make sure they were even. He looked at Tess for an answer and something about the question in his eyes made the force of

Jamie knock down the mask she had fought so recently to hide behind.

"Sight for sore eyes," she assured him.

Relieved, he grinned straight at her. Poe clicked off a shot. The noise of the shutter startled Jamie, and he straightened up into a Buck Campbell pose, upright as a pine. His look was slyly earnest, full of charm. Poe snapped several shots in succession, but he wanted more of what he had seen in that first frame, more of that intimacy.

"Keep talking," Poe instructed Tess in a fervent whisper. His narrow fingers were flying all over his equipment. He was in perpetual motion, yet there was something still about him. "Let me see him as you do."

"Tell me about where you grew up," Tess asked Buck, as casually as if they were strangers.

"Little town just across the border from here, in Arkansas. Little place called Prosperity."

"Miss it?"

"Sure do," he said. "You always miss the place where you learned to drive and where you played ball and where you fell in love." He looked shy suddenly. And wistful. He lowered his eyes. When he raised his head, he found her eyes again, his own gray eyes smoldering with something more than mere nostalgia. Poe snapped furiously.

"Prosperity," she said. "Ever go back?"

"Nobody there for me anymore," he said, his sadness looming over him.

"Oh," Tess said. "Was there someone special?"

A wave of emotion went over the star's face as he looked beyond her to the trees glowing brilliantly green in the pure, honeyed light of late afternoon: sadness and regret and finally—as his

70

eyes came back to hers—joy. "You know it," he said, laying his fine hand over the place where his heart was beating.

Poe practically bleated in his euphoria.

CHAPTER EIGHT

That night, Buck Campbell was performing at the Wayne Newton Theater, splitting the show with Newton himself.

Tess swung by the hotel and picked Poe up. He was in an elevated state, and she welcomed his giddiness as a distraction from the urgency coursing through her. Today she had fleetingly been with the only man she had truly loved. And then he had slipped back into the mists that had held him for more than a decade. So, as she clutched the steering wheel, it seemed that she had never greeted anyone with as much gratitude as she now felt for Poe. He seemed an anchor.

"You're good," he said to her admiringly. "You're amazing."

She laughed. "What's that supposed to mean?"

"The way you seduced him," he enthused.

"Excuse me?" she sputtered.

Poe shrugged, and then waved his delicate hands in the air to evoke his point. "Maybe you wouldn't want to call it seduction. Myself, I think it was more."

"What?"

"His soul calling to yours."

She laughed again.

"Don't laugh," he said solemnly, almost eerily. "I have seen these things. I know they exist."

"What exists?"

"Maybe you won't wanna believe me. but I saw that his soul quickened to yours. I saw that the two of you have known each other in another life."

As the hair at the nape of her neck tingled, she laughed. It was laughter that fizzed up out of some spring deep within, spilled along the cleft that Jamie's voice had opened. Her laughter soothed her, coursing gingerly along the tender rend in her heart. It felt so good she couldn't stop, and Poe seemed bemused by it, not hurt.

"You laugh," he said, smiling at her knowingly. "Maybe you don't remember it, but long ago when he was someone else and you were someone else. The soul doesn't forget."

"Oh, Poe," she said.

"See," he said, pointing to the fine hair on her arms that had been called up by the strange insight of his words. "Your body is starting to remember. See, you have gooseflesh."

"That's not a nice thing to say," she teased him as the car crawled through the preconcert traffic. "*Goose*flesh."

"I wanna work with you again," Poe told her, dispensing with his otherworldly observations. "I'm telling the people at the magazine: Send me with Tess Boone." His tone was grand.

"You're too kind," she said, trying to disguise an embarrassed delight that somebody had witnessed her bond with Jamie.

She turned into the circle drive at the theater and wound up by the racehorse sculpture and fountain, where she waved away the valet who offered to park the car. Valets in the Ozark Mountains! Even the fans here were a more spangled crowd. Rhinestones flashed in the late sun. Stiletto heels sunk into the squishy asphalt. Poe was gaping at the spectacle. "Wayniacs," Tess explained as they waited for a group of women to move past an open parking place. "Wayne Newton's fans get dolled up and make pilgrimages here in droves." Poe merely shook his head in astonishment.

After parking, Tess insisted on helping Poe with his heavy bags. The photographer protested at first but relented as the heat wavering up off the asphalt blasted him. Tess draped a bag of lights over her shoulder, and the two slogged their way across the lot behind a Wayniac in a strapless sequin gown and nosebleed high heels. As she teetered along, the woman clung to her escort in his rented tuxedo. Suddenly, she stopped, swayed on the perch of her shoes, and sniffed the evening air, as if to marshal every sense into the preservation of this superlative moment.

"Do you smell cow manure?" she said, searching the air with her nostrils. Her companion looked around until he spotted a bull grazing in the neighboring field. He pointed, and his lady exhaled her disdain.

Tess cracked up as she and Poe circled the couple. "Welcome to Branson," she muttered under her breath, suddenly proud of the way the renegade spirit of the mountains was holding its own against the encroaching neon.

Even Poe got the irony of it all, and they were still laughing when they emerged into the lobby with its white columns and banisters. Tess spotted Lisbeth and Georgia standing to one side of the balcony, surveying the scene in the rotunda. Before Tess could avert her eyes, Lisbeth waved her over. Leaving Poe to guard his heap of equipment, Tess made her way over to the two women.

"Feeling better?" Lisbeth asked in her affable way.

"Sure," Tess said. "Thanks." But she was thinking, *Is there anybody who hasn't heard that I ditched out last night?*

"A new form of homesickness," Lisbeth offered. "You get sick when you get home."

Some sort of canny radar seemed to kick in. Georgia looked at Tess with new scrutiny. "You're from around here?"

"Born and bred," Tess replied, hoping she would be nimble enough to dance away from any implicating details.

"Where'd you say?" Lisbeth pressed, genuinely trying to prod her own fading memory of their introductory phone conversation earlier in the week.

Tess didn't want to say; she wanted to be vague. But she also didn't want to act suspicious or downright lie. She thought of saying Blue Eye or Mountain Home. What she finally said was broader and still the truth: "Arkansas."

"Where?" Georgia probed.

"Just a tiny spot, near the border here. I've been hoping to catch a few minutes to chase down there, and see how it's changed. I haven't been home since my father's funeral."

"When are you leaving?" Lisbeth asked.

"Tomorrow morning," Tess said. "Though I may stretch it out a bit if I can, just dart over the line before heading back up to the airport. It's too tempting." Terribly aware that Georgia's eyes were fixed unblinkingly on her, Tess swerved onto the safer topic of the T-shirt featuring Buck Campbell's backside. She talked a little too glibly, a little too quickly. Her one hope was that Georgia didn't know her well enough to know that she was hiding something.

It worked: Georgia's expression lifted, brightened. "Those shirts outsell the others four to one," she said. "We can't keep enough of them." Then, abruptly, she made a move to go. "So we'll see you backstage tonight," she informed Tess. "For one last session."

Tess nodded. "One last session."

"Don't be late. We won't have long. We're leaving at dawn. Buck's got a recording session before the world tour kicks in."

"Okay." Tess's tone was calm, even though the word "dawn" was echoing clangorously inside her.

With that, Georgia followed the corridor that led backstage. Heather Trace tried to intercept her. Georgia made the barest pause, shook her head emphatically, moved on.

Lisbeth suppressed a stage shudder, and Tess swapped wry grins with her.

Tess was laughing when they parted, but she felt an ache inside. She had known the end was coming, that he would leave and she would go back to New York. But she hadn't been looking it full in the face. She had been concentrating on tonight, on sitting in that dark theater and hearing him sing. She hadn't thought past that final interview, those last few minutes.

And then he was all there was in the world again. He was in the light, singing. His voice made the ache radiate out from her heart so that every note he sang throbbed with her losing him again.

The show was different tonight. For half of it, he sat on a barstool in a lone spotlight, cradling his old guitar. He sang the slow love songs that he had loved as a boy when she was his only audience. He sang the funny songs that used to make her laugh. They still did. She sat with a smile on her face. A strange sensation was chasing through the crowd. This was a Buck Campbell they had never seen. They sat forward, leaning into him, magnetized and mystified. But Tess knew: This was Jamie, her Jamie.

He spoke. It was not something Buck Campbell did much on stage, if ever. He let his music say it all. But tonight he looked up into the spotlight, he looked out across his audience, and he began to speak. "If you live your life on the road, the way I do," he began, "you eat hundred-year-old sourdough biscuits on Route 66 down in New Mexico, and you watch the water come rushing over Niagara Falls, and you watch a hawk just float over the Grand Canyon. You get distracted by California redwoods and buildings made of mirrors that reflect the clouds because they're so high up there in the sky. And you can distract yourself from not being where you really wanna be, which is home." He strummed on the guitar a little. "I grew up here." He grinned, punctuating his thought. "Well, just over the state line from here. But you know home's not so much a bunch of trees or houses or even a certain creek. And to tell you the truth, I had given up hope of ever making it back."

He played some chords on the guitar, a little

melody mixed in. And when he looked up again, his eyes glistened in the spotlight. "I believe in angels," he said. "This is for the one who brought me home again."

It was a Willie Nelson song, and Jamie sang it with sweetness and forgiveness. He sang it with a love that cracked his voice a little: *If you had not have fallen, I would not have found you, angel flying too close to the ground. Fly on, fly on past the speed of sound. I'd rather see you up than see you down. Leave me if you need to, I will still remember, angel flying too close to the ground.*

There were only two people in this moment, inside the clasp of the song, though it was witnessed by thousands. Tess sat shivering in the warm rush of it. Jamie couldn't see her, but he knew she was there. She could hear him, and he could hear her answering heart. She knew he could.

And then Buck Campbell was back for a rousing finale. He danced a two-step with his guitar and kicked high and mighty. Tess slipped into the aisle, wanting to get herself knitted back together before she had to go backstage and see him, see him with Georgia. But as she neared the back row, Georgia emerged like a specter out of the dusk. She took hold of Tess's arm and guided her to the back wall of the theater, where they stood together, watching the one moving figure on stage.

The crowd called for an encore, and Buck returned and played some killer guitar. Without moving her gaze from the stage, Georgia said, "Where did you say you were from?"

Rebellion bayed up in Tess, a will to own the

moment, the gift Jamie had just given her. She wanted this woman to know that he loved her, Tess. She didn't care whom it hurt—Georgia, Jamie, herself. He might not belong to her anymore, but the moment just passed did belong to her. "Prosperity," Tess answered.

They stood in the silence between them as the music pounded up and down the walls, crashed down from the ceilings. The amber light from the stage reflected on both their faces, but neither turned to look at the other.

When the curtain fell, Georgia strode off with purpose.

CHAPTER NINE

After Wayne Newton had smoothly thrilled his fans and after the final curtain had been drawn, Tess and Poe were turned away from their backstage visit. No reason was given. Though of course Tess knew why. The mild photographer was frothing over it, the quietest tempest she had ever witnessed. "How dare she?" he said as if repeating a mantra. Tess was reminded again how entitled New Yorkers thought they were. They always expected every door should open to them, and if it didn't, they were appalled—and persistent. Maybe it was justifiable. After all, they put up with subway fires causing delays and cabbies who smoked and elevators that got stuck between floors. She felt strangely detached as she listened to Poe fume, suspended somewhere above him, observing him.

"I didn't perceive she had the proper kind of eyes to see," Poe said spookily. "But, that wife, she saw what you had been. That must be it, why else?" Now he was mixing his own Eastern-tinged religion with the New York penchant for doing autopsies on recent events. People in the city indulged incessantly; they were masters of the postmortem.

"I've got enough," Tess said, meaning enough to write a story, although she couldn't even think that far ahead and was only saying it to say *something*. The one word she had spoken to Georgia had banished Tess to some faraway purgatory. She could not bring herself back. She felt like she and Poe were at opposite ends of a string with two tin cans knotted at each end. She couldn't quite hear him, couldn't quite care enough to hear him, and felt she had to catapult her voice to his ear.

Tess pulled up to the hotel where Poe was staying. She held out her hand to him, and attempted a sincere tone of voice: "It was good to work with you. Have a good flight tomorrow."

His face fell, and he said, "I thought we were on the same flight back to New York."

"I'm gonna grab a later one. I've got something to do." She could tell it made him peevish. Now he was going to have to ride the hotel van to the airport—with the tourists. But he held her hand in a long farewell clasp, as though all were forgiven. He tried once again to get her to grab a bite to eat with him now; he'd turned up a little place that actually would tailor a vegetarian meal. She declined, said goodbye, and part of her was sorry because really, compared to some of the arrogant paparazzi she had worked with, Poe was an intriguing character. On another assignment, he would have been diverting. They might even have become friends. He seemed a misfit, and in New York she had accumulated a clutch of friends who found the city liberating after the places they had been before—a gay romance novelist from North Carolina, a SoHo artist who was trying to scrub New Jersey from under her nails, a Greek Orthodox librarian who had hated marriage but loved sex. Tess could see Poe at one of her supper gatherings, counseling someone in a corner about his guru. But, after this, she would fear seeing him, fear the image that he would call up, the phantom of Jamie in his Stetson with love in his eyes. These things coursed fluidly through her mind and then were swept away by a tidal wash of Jamie. Her thoughts of him rushed clamorously upon her as she drove out of the canopy of reflected light over Branson, back out to where the stars shown.

It was over. Her work was complete. Her time with Jamie was gone. She had slammed the door on their reunion. She wondered if he would feel betrayed by her refusal to answer Georgia's question with a lie. How could he? He had brought his love exposed and vulnerable onto the stage. He had shown himself to thousands of people, and to his wife. In how many ways would Georgia make him suffer for it? How would it change what they shared? What was there to change?

Tess couldn't let herself dwell on it. She had to find her way back to the silence that she lived inside, the quiet denial that had let her leave Prosperity and allowed her to ascend to the top of her field. She had to find a way back to her life. This had been a dangerous diversion. She had found Jamie, found herself, found home. But at what price to the life she had made for herself? She couldn't let herself be unhinged by this.

She turned up the radio. It was Willie Nelson singing "Blue Eyes Crying in the Rain." It was sad and sweet and reminded her of Jamie's song to her tonight. They had always loved the unlikely poetry in Willie Nelson's songs, loved the rough ribbon of his voice as it unspooled onto the night air. She reached to flick off the radio but couldn't follow through, vowing instead that this was the last minute she was ever going to listen to country music again in her life. She swore it. Tomorrow she would go home to Prosperity, just to see it again. And then she would leave for New York and her $1,600 one-bedroom apartment and her salmon dinners at East Side trattorias. She would return to the men in Barneys ties whom friends met at benefits and thought of her. From now on, Tess would only listen to Johnny Hartman and John Coltrane doing "Lush Life." She would only listen to WNYC playing Handel and Mozart. Just as Jamie would go home to Buck Campbell and Georgia and recording studios and a Christmas special on ABC. The time she and Jamie had reclaimed together, what they now knew was still there inside them, would burrow deep within them again, where it wouldn't hurt them, where they would no longer see-feel-taste-hear-smell what they were missing every day of their lives.

It belonged to another lifetime.

CHAPTER TEN

Tess comforted herself with a custom she often indulged at home in her apartment above Broadway. She kindled candles. The flames were like other presences in the room. Tonight they made her feel not so alone. The shadows danced along the walls, tricking at least her eye into believing she was not completely abandoned to the storm in her heart. She put on a silk tank and boxers, and she drank a glass of chardonnay and surrendered herself to drift in the current of what had happened to her in the past two days. Only two days, she thought, but she had traveled the whole distance of her life in their span of hours. She roiled with emotion. She longed to have back her peace again, the calm she felt in New York. For so long, she had only observed life, as though she were above, looking down upon it. It had been her job; it had been her way of life. Often, she had joked to her friends that she was an anthropologist, determined not to go native. She would watch the people who lived around her in New York, as she had watched the people in her hometown. She would not really get involved, not deeply. It was torpor really, emotional torpor. But she could at least live that way.

The hours fell away, and she was aware of the very minutes passing. She could not keep herself from feeling that these were the last moments she and Jamie would be in the same place, in the same time zone even. From here, the divide would only grow. From the moment he had sung to her from the stage with tears in his eyes, the chasm between them had inched wider and wider. The embrace of that song, mere notes vibrating in air, was as close as they would come. She paced the room to try to spin off some of what was inside her. She drew a Jacuzzi but couldn't get in. She thought of driving down to Prosperity tonight, just getting in the car and going. But after the chardonnay, she didn't trust herself.

To escape, Tess tossed the quilt around her shoulders and went out into the night. It throbbed with the instruments of insects. A breeze was sighing up high in the pines. Barefoot, she walked on the cushion of the path that led down to the sand at the lake's edge. The moon was still low enough to be infused with the golden glow of the sun on the far side of the earth. It reflected sepia sunlight across the waters. Tess looked up from the lake to survey the constellations. She had never learned their names. Maybe it was because, in the beginning, she didn't want to gaze up at them and hear any other than his name. But many times, when she had escaped New York on assignment, she had gone out and looked up to see what he would see if he looked up to see what she would see. Honestly, though, thinking back, she wasn't sure she had acknowledged anymore—or ever in all those years—that she was doing it in his memory. It had simply become a part of her, as he had become a part of her past too painful to admit, too painful to recall even as she stood searching for the brightest star, searching from Canada or Provence or down along the Gulf Coast.

Tess smelled the oaken spice of him just as she

felt his arms slip around her from behind. Her skin prickled as if reaching for him with every molecule of her being. Her knees gave, and she could only sway into him, letting him take her weight. He held her in his strong arms, the safe circle of his strong arms. She couldn't see his face, but she reached for his hand, the warm papery grasp of his palm, and held it tight. The two of them stayed that way, both of their faces turned toward the lake full of reflected stars.

Finally, he turned her around to face him, searching her eyes.

The night had taken the color out of the world. But his eyes were still gray. The lashes were still too delicate in the rough cut of his face. Those eyes softened his edge. They always spoke silently for him. And honestly.

He pulled her close and the warmth of him began to seep through her light clothes and then through her chilled skin; it moved through her, into her bloodstream. He was like wine having its way.

He was all the past, and suddenly they were nothing but who they had been. All else that they had been and had become fell away. Everywhere they had been since they had last stood like this was gone. They were only the memory of what they had been together. They had never parted. She had never forced their parting. They had always been like this, two kids with the whole Milky Way orbiting slowly around them.

Time fell away, all the seasons between, and with the beating of their hearts, the clocks began again within them that had stopped years before. His heart drummed steadily against her, its rhythm the backbeat in the song that sung through her. Hers beat in harmony. They seemed all heartbeat, all vibration. She reached tighter around his narrow waist and breathed him in. He stroked her hair, then brought his lips down, brushed them along her ear, breathing low: "Come with me."

"Where?" she whispered into his kiss.

"Just come," he said.

He waited on the porch as she dressed, snuffed the candles, threw her things together. When she came back into the dark, he shouldered her bag and took her hand. They slipped together through the resort, staying in the night shade of the trees until they emerged into a clearing where a helicopter hulked blackly.

Tess stopped Jamie. "What . . . ?"

"It's Wayne's," he said. "It's okay." He led her on, walking swiftly.

They climbed into the chopper. The pilot nodded an acknowledgment and then turned to his work. The blades turned, thudding against the night air. In the light of the control panel, Tess could see Jamie's face clearly for the first time. His jaw was set, his skin flushed with defiance. He kept her hand cradled in his.

They passed Branson laid out like bright jewels on black satin, then flew over the foil-like stretches of the glimmering lake and into the hills that loomed like shadows against the moon-blue sky. They didn't talk over the chop of the rotors, and Tess felt somehow outside herself. Always the haughty observer of celebrity, the outsider, Tess was aware, though numbly, that she had moved over into the inner sanctum. She was a journalist who had just become a story she could never tell. She had just chosen to become a story that another reporter could sell magazines with, and lots of them. She thought of Heather, but the thought moved through her mind quickly as a traveler making connections in an airport and then was gone. Heather didn't exist, nor Logan. Her magazine didn't. His wife didn't. There was only this man who had come for her with no words and said everything she needed to hear.

The pilot set them down in a clearing. Light spilled in yellow squares from the windows of a cottage at the edge of the woods. Jamie clambered down and lifted her out. He saluted the pilot and then encircled Tess with his arm as they stood in the whirlpooling air of the helicopter's ascent. It beat like a heart.

They stood until the sound grew faint and disappeared, although Tess couldn't be sure when exactly that happened because it was so like the thrumming of blood in her ears. Jamie brought her around at last so that he could see into her by starlight. He touched her face, his fingers playing over her as though he thought he could call music from her skin. He bent toward her and brushed her lips with his, lightly, before moving away and holding her in his sight. She stirred up toward him, responding to a reflexive magnetism. But he didn't answer her movement again. For long moments, he gazed down on her, his fingers caressing. She wept, and her tears ran through his fingers.

Finally, he caught her up and pressed her against him, lifted her off her feet. Her eyes were closed on their flood, but she thought that if she opened them, the whole universe would be circling round them again. Jamie kissed her full then, drank her in. It called up a terrible thirst in her, startling her. Something, everything in her answered his desire, her own desire materializing like an apparition of remembered sensation. She had not felt in all their time apart what now washed over her like memory itself. She had forgotten how hot blood could run, how it could flood like effervescent molten metal all through you, how you could feel yourself melting. And as she dissolved, the years between them disappeared and were utterly gone. They were not two lovers who had lost each other for time. They were the two lovers they had been, two kids who had needed each other, who had shielded each other from the churlish circumstances they were given. There was no yesterday, no tomorrow. There was only always and this moment that contained it wholly.

Tess yearned toward him, ached toward him, as they gently sank down into the pine needles cushioning the ground. She was so still as he settled his face against hers, as he ran his hand gingerly along the curve of her body, as if he were stroking the strings of his guitar. She began to answer him, move with him, as he loomed over her, rising and falling on her breath. She hid her face in the tangle of hair in the hollow of his chest, and they fell together into some timeless, bottomless place, fell together until she lay covered by his heft, secure, anchored, home.

"I love you," he whispered into her arching neck. Again, into the fall of hair across her shoulder, "I love you." And again, "I love you" into the hollow between her breasts. He rose above her and said it aloud so that it seemed to carry across the hills, to resound off the bluffs.

The clamor of crickets hushed at his words.

And she put a finger against his lips. "Shh," she said, and rose to kiss him. "I love you," she said into his parted lips as they greeted hers.

CHAPTER ELEVEN

Jamie carried her into the cottage. The room was softly flushed with the light of candles flickering in bowls of thick Mexican glass. He settled her on the four-poster bed that dominated the room. "Where are we?" she asked as he opened a refrigerator and brought a bottle of Perrier back to the bed. "I feel like Alice through the looking glass."

His face was ruddy. His shoulders were wide. He had pine needles in his hair. He came back to her, climbed up next to her on the bed, poured her a glass of sparkling water. "Wayne's guest place," he said. "We're old buddies." He shrugged. "As old as buddies get in this business."

"What did you tell him? What did you tell *her?*" she asked, unable to refer to his wife by name.

"What does it matter?" he said as he leaned down to kiss her lingeringly. Then he pulled back and fixed her with a mock-serious look. "This is off the record, you know."

She bit the tip of his nose lightly.

He went on: "I don't want you writing some story with a title like 'Buck Naked.'"

"You have to say off the record before you say or do what you don't want printed. It's not retroactive."

"So I can't take it back."

"Nope."

"I don't want to," he said, gathering her to him. They were quiet. She picked the pine needles out of his hair, ran them along his arm. Finally, he spoke: "You have some apologizing to do."

"So do you."

"Where do you want me to start?" he asked, moving his lips across her eyebrows.

"Right there," she murmured as he kissed the freckles on her nose. It dulled her sense of some vague fear, gnawing. She began to forget again that anyone or anything existed beyond him, beyond this moment.

When he brought his mouth back to hers, she savored the taste of him, the sweetness she had discovered when she was so young and which had mellowed and become more dear with the passage of time. She was intoxicated by him. How had she ever given him up?

"I'm sorry," she said, grabbing him to her tightly. "I'm sorry." She didn't mean for what she had said to Georgia tonight. She didn't mean for being the reason he had played loose with his life to be with her now. She meant for long ago, for what she had done that had brought them around to this. She lapsed into the past. "Where'd you go—when you left?"

"To hell," he said, smirking and reaching for a strand of hair that was caught in the corner of her mouth.

"Maybe I don't want to know." Her voice carried a lot of pent-up misery she hadn't let out to air for years.

"It wasn't so bad. I drifted south. I was sleeping

in that truck, trying to drink enough so the world looked little. Down in Tennessee, I got beat up real bad one night and woke up in jail the next morning. And I ended up staying in there for weeks 'cause I didn't have any money to get out. It was filthy as sin. Cockroaches scurrying all over and stuff growing in the toilets." He shuddered at the memory.

"Basically, I just crawled on my belly for a couple of years, and then I got settled down in a little town outside of Nashville. Friendly guy owned a bar there. He used to sing a lot, and I started in singing with him. First time since I was with you. And it felt good. I had my guitar with me, wasn't worth pawning, and besides I couldn't part with it because it was the only thing I could put my hands on that came from you. I sang those real achy-heart songs. Used to make people cry in their Bud singin' "I'm So Lonesome I Could Die.""

He looked at her and crooked an eyebrow. "I coulda too," he said.

"You could've what?"

"Coulda died from lonesome." He yodeled a little on the end of it. He was ignoring what haunted them both. He was ignoring the specter of his wife.

And Tess found she was so grateful to him for it that she began to laugh, igniting laughter in him so that he pulled her up into his lap and held her there. "Tessie," he said, nuzzling her until they hushed into solemnity.

She cradled his moist head in the crook of her arm and smoothed his fine hair away from his ears, away from the high slope of his forehead. She brushed her lips along the tender bit of flesh at his temple and murmured that she loved him. She kissed the little scar at the edge of his right eyebrow and told him again how she loved him. She nibbled at his cheekbone. She ran her lips over his eyelids. "I love you," she said. "I love you."

"Have you ever been back?" he asked her quietly.

She shook her head. "You?"

"I never could bring myself to go back," he said. "I knew you wouldn't be there. And the Calhouns've been gone so long now."

She wanted to ask again how he was managing this and how long he could sustain it. But she couldn't bring herself to ambush their happiness with reminders that it was merely stolen. She judged he was reminded, even as she was, judged by the sudden way he caught her to him. He clasped her desperately then, and the smile went out of his eyes. They burned, kissing each other as if the intensity of their love could solder together what they had conspired all these years to keep apart.

"Tessie," he whispered like water rushing over gravel. "I've never stopped looking up at the stars and thinking of you."

She laced her fingers up with his just as she laced every fiber to his, binding them together as though there would never come another moment when she would once again be set free to resume the course she had chosen when she was still a girl in an old football jersey lying in bed and dreaming how she would walk away from the only home she had ever known, would ever know.

The insects throbbed around them, sentinels in the night. The candles burned down and extinguished themselves in a spiritlike breath of smoke that curled up and disappeared. The sky grew pink in the east. All the while, she and Jamie loved each other as they had always loved each other—to the exclusion of what waited for him beyond the clearing, beyond the trees, beyond her arms.

CHAPTER TWELVE

When they woke, Jamie's grin was as big as morning. There was no trace of Buck Campbell about him. They got up and drank brewed coffee. A lavish breakfast—waffles and berries and orange juice rich with pulp—arrived from the main house. They sat in the sun on Adirondack chairs, their bare feet touching in the grass. Jamie looked like the boy she had known back home—a denim shirt with a gray tee under it, faded jeans, even an Arkansas Razorbacks ball cap.

"When do we leave?" he asked her.

"Where are we going?"

"Home," he said.

Tess stared at him as the birds twittered in high branches. She wanted more than anything to just take this on faith. She wanted just to go to Prosperity with him, enjoy this time together and not wonder. But she couldn't; it was impossible. "I need to understand this," she told him.

"Understand what?" he asked as she searched his bright face. "I'm here."

"I see that," she said. "How are you here?"

He shrugged the question aside brusquely. "I'm here, Tess."

She drew her legs up under her in the chair, crossed her arms. It was a pose that said she meant to stay there until he talked. "I need to understand, Jamie. It's a girl thing."

"Are you sure it's not a journalist thing?" he said, softening his words by pulling her up to her feet, holding her close to him. He was warm as summer.

He slipped his finger inside a coil of hair, which was still wet from the shower they had shared. It gleamed like copper wire as it wound up his finger. "Nothing dries hair faster than wind," he told her and kissed her forehead. "Come on."

The phone pulsed from inside the house: once, twice, a third time. She studied his face. He didn't acknowledge the summons of the phone, of the world.

"Okay," she told him. "Let's go."

They loaded into an old truck with worn seats and a muddled paint job. "It'll fit right into Prosperity," he said.

"Are you sure it'll make it that far?" Tess asked incredulously.

Jamie winked. "It's got a secret."

Tess waited as Jamie turned the key. The old truck sputtered, then purred. "You can't judge everything by the cow dung on its mud flaps," he told her pointedly. "Under the hood, it's a whole different machine."

Jamie rolled down his window, adjusted the mirrors, and then gazed over at her. "How am I gonna drive?" he asked her in a low voice. "Tessie, all I wanna do is look at you."

He pulled her over to sit next to him, wedged

up against the gearshift. "Let's make the two-headed monster," he said, reminding her of the way their friends had dubbed them that because she always rode shoulder-to-shoulder with him when he was driving.

"Oh, Jamie," she said, and ran her fingers along the sandpaper of his chin. He leaned over to meet her lips.

She studied him then, the dear angles of his face that time had not changed, the curl of his lashes, the even brow. Her pleasure in it was marred, though. "Your face," she said, touching his cheek. "What if somebody sees us?"

"Nobody's gonna recognize me. I look too happy to be Buck Campbell." He raced the truck's engine before steering slowly along the curving road that wound away from the main house, which Tess could see crowning a swell of land. Emmylou Harris was singing "Prayer in Open D" on the radio, and Jamie was humming along. But as reminiscent as it all was of blissful hours spent together, Tess couldn't staunch a sense of dread that was trickling into her. How were they here together? By what means?

She watched the lake spark, a robin jump in the grass, the cottony clouds scudding along in the blue, blue sky. Finally Jamie turned onto the back road that ran across the state line to Prosperity. He opened up the speed. Several times, he glanced over as if to spy what was going on inside her. But really, she thought, he must know.

He must know that she was used to getting answers, that she couldn't, even in the name of love or maybe especially, suspend her need to understand about his life, about the part of the past they hadn't shared. And yet he seemed to feel no inclination to tell her. There was a stony resolve about him that she had never seen before, that had perhaps come inevitably with celebrity, with always having so many people wanting so many things from you. But what she wanted from him was not so much, only to be told where he had been and how he felt about the woman who had taken him there, or at least accompanied him. Maybe, Tess thought, and it pained her to think it, maybe he had learned at last to protect himself, even from her, even from someone who loved him so much.

Because love hadn't been enough the last time, had it? Her hand resting now on his leg reminded her of how it had rested there when they were young and driving up to the lake or down to the river or just driving. Back then, his sad songs had moved through the cab of the truck with the wind blowing warm across their faces. And even as Tess had felt the steel of his thigh through his denim jeans, she had known how easy it would be to hurt him. Recognizing that hadn't kept her from it—had only made her suffer it more.

The trees ticked off at the roadside as the old Ford sped along through cloud shadows on the pavement, in and out of the sunshine, the shadows.

He looked over at her again, picked up her hand and held it on the gearshift, tracing her fingers with his.

"Just tell me," she said quietly, "just tell me how you managed this. I mean today."

He exhaled as though he had been holding his breath since the last time they were together, and that the burden of her questioning him was more than he could bear. When he spoke, it was in a tone that hurt her to hear: "I didn't ask her permission if that's what you mean."

"Sorry," Tess said. "I didn't mean it that way."

"Look, Tess, if it weren't for her, I don't know who I'd be by now."

"I'd settle for Jamie."

"You didn't settle for Jamie, though, did you?"

Tears rushed into her eyes. Her lips quivered. Part of her fought it fiercely, but the old part of her, the girl who loved him so much and wanted nothing to harm him ever, couldn't hold in her shame and her confusion and her longing just to have it all be again as it once was, and now never could be. Not purely.

"Oh, God, Tessie," he said, pulling her hand up to hold it against his face. "I didn't mean to say that. I didn't mean to ruin things."

"Neither did I," she said, and pressed her face against the rough weave of his shirt. She wept then for Jamie and for herself and even for Georgia; wept because life was a cruel shifting business, and sometimes things worked out successfully, beautifully, but not for the best. Because sometimes your heart was filled with regret, but not enough to change the past—not even a moment of it.

CHAPTER THIRTEEN

"Don't cry," Jamie said at last. "Don't cry, honey. We're going home."

Tess kept her face on his shoulder, rubbing the

96

muscle in his arm as though she could change everything with the force of wanting to. She was sniffling, trying to wrestle herself back together. The ground had been shifting under her feet ever since that first night she had walked in and heard Buck Campbell singing in Jamie's voice. She had not cried in years, but this weekend she had cried an Arkansas spring shower, a real gully washer, as Jamie would say. And she wasn't sure she could completely stop now that she was started. New York wasn't a place that countenanced tears. You got trampled over, left behind if you cried. If tears crept up on you, you had to close the door and bolt it twice. Tess had learned that locks in the city aren't just to keep out the muggers and the druggies. Locks are to hide behind, to hold back the world because if you show your weakness out on the street or in the green fluorescent light of the office, you're finished. Tess hadn't cried in someone else's presence in more than a decade. In fact, she couldn't remember when last she had cried at all.

"Look," Jamie said. "You can see the bluffs above the creek."

She straightened up and looked at the steely bluffs rising roughly along the serpentine treeline that followed the creek. Dogwoods ruffled along the top of the bluffs, edged by the pink of redbuds. Tess squeezed his hand, but didn't speak. It was beyond words how good it felt to see the familiar terrain, how good it felt for her to be riding along as somebody she trusted took the wheel. Not just in the driving sense. She could feel herself relaxing completely into Jamie's care, giving the burden to him.

Ahead of them, the church steeple pierced the

tree line, and as they crested the next ridge, the town rose up whole before them, nestled in the valley along a crook in the road. To the south, Sugar Creek hugged it in a wide arc. To the north, Stones Throw Mountain rose.

Jamie drove down Main Street. Kimball's Grocery still had its worn-plank porch, and there were several old guys whittling away Sunday morning with idle talk. The yards were neat and daffodils lined most of the front sidewalks, which were knocked into crazy angles by the roots of the old maples. Trees were flowering by every rock cottage and every worn, gabled Victorian.

"The Dairy Creme," he said wistfully as they passed the squat corner building with its screen windows where Tess had often ordered a twist cone and paid a dime for it. They passed the bank with its gold lettering on the door. It had marble floors inside and exquisitely carved maple woodwork. Her grandfather had turned the spindles that framed the teller's face. Tess had always loved to go there on an errand while Mama was down at Kimball's or over at the café. Even in summer, it was cool inside the bank and smelled of paper. It returned to her, the feeling of moving along these sidewalks, going into the bank, the store, the café. She had never felt alone. One pair of eyes had carried her to the next, as if the whole town shared one optic nerve: Spinster Ada Banks watched from her porch until Tess passed by the knotted elm, whereupon she moved into the view of her mama's friend Stella, who was doing dishes and monitoring the world out her kitchen window. From Stella's sight, Tess walked beyond the lilac bushes to where Old Mac could watch her past his body shop as he spit tobacco on the stained slab of concrete where he had been spitting it since her father loafed there as a boy. Wherever she had gone in Prosperity, she had moved along an intangible web that somehow connected her with everyone else. Everyone knew her, knew whose daughter she was, whose grand-daughter. It was a safe feeling, but it had been uncomfortable in the end because as she had grown up and started distinguishing herself at school by getting the highest grades and by winning state poetry contests, she had started to feel the scrutiny of those who watched. It didn't seem benign and neighborly anymore. It seemed almost that they were watching for her to fall and prove them all right in their cherished notion that a person should settle in with the crowd, that a person shouldn't have her name in the paper but three times—at birth, at marriage, at death. And so even now as Tess looked with affection upon the town she still called home, she rememбеed why she had ached to leave.

Being here with Jamie heightened her sense of what had gone, who had slipped away. She saw herself, saw the two of them driving this road with the windows down in summer or through snowstorms, in a pounding rain or in still, still midnight. They were sixteen and seventeen and eighteen, driving where she had gone with her father, where Pop's father had gone before them. They had all passed this way so many times and so many times since in her memory.

They wound out of town, over the bridge, out past the old brick high school with its high windows. Just looking at it, Tess could smell the floor polish and the dusty rows of books in the library. She could hear the thunder the building made when a herd of kids took off at the bell and raced down the stairs for freedom. Jamie pulled into the deserted parking lot with the football stadium behind it. The stadium seemed so much smaller, so dilapidated, though they concluded that it hadn't changed since last they were here. It still had the same cardinal mascot painted above the concession stand, and Tess wondered how many Augusts a new Pep Club chairman had traced over the old design with new red and blue and yellow paint.

"Where do we go?" Jamie asked as the truck idled at the lip of the parking lot exit. They looked at each other. She saw a knot working at the hinge of his jaw. This was home, but coming back wasn't altogether easy. She had family here, on her mother's side, though nobody she did more than send a Christmas card to every year. Her cousin Lou did remember her birthday every year. But as a whole, that side of the family had thought her college education uppity. Her father's family was gone. And Jamie had nobody.

"Let's go to the cemetery," she said.

The Baptist church was weathering. It needed fresh paint. And the yard wasn't trimmed up as nice as Tess remembered. The gravel parking lot was lined with a dozen cars and trucks, nothing new, just reliable, long vehicles with paint jobs so old they looked dusty. Tess and Jamie had to pass by the tall windows of the sanctuary to get to the cemetery in the shady backyard. She vaguely hoped the brim of her straw hat would disguise her face. Jamie was harder to hide. Who wouldn't remember his long stride? The whole county had watched him move on the football field, the basketball court. They had watched him on the country music channel, on the Grammys. But he just took her hand and strolled past, as though they were two tourists passing through, maybe doing some work on the family genealogy.

They walked among the family plots, the names reading like a roll call of their youth, calling up the old faces so that Tess felt as though they moved through a crowd who greeted their homecoming. Jamie was quiet as he pulled a couple of weeds away from the Calhouns' gravestone, and Tess felt her heart inside her as she cast her eyes in the southwest corner, looking for the name she knew best. She found it at last, under a dogwood in bloom. The white blossoms on the tree were its only adornment; no one had recently decorated the grave.

"I should've brought some flowers," she said hoarsely as she stood over Pop's grave. His name didn't look like it belonged engraved in stone. She remembered it written in his own hand on the inside cover of each of his books, on the application to the university that he never sent: Samuel David Boone. Otherwise, he was just Pop.

Tears were burning at the back of her eyes again. Jamie came closer, and she looked up at him hoping he knew how sorry Pop had been. His ball cap cut a shadow across his face.

"You okay?" she asked.

He didn't answer at first, but finally said, "It's just bringing it all back. And I don't want it back—not all of it."

She leaned into him, and he into her, until all that held them up was their embrace, their union. Nothing more.

They stood that way in the shade for a while longer. Inside the church, the congregation began to sing. A hymn floated out of the church windows, the voices that carried it thin but sweet on the breeze: *Amazing grace, how sweet the sound, that saved a wretch like me. I once was lost, but now am found, was blind but now I see.*

CHAPTER FOURTEEN

They went into Kimball's and bought Cokes in green bottles and Hershey's with almonds. Jess Kimball, who was nudging eighty hard, didn't make out their faces or maybe didn't notice that those faces had been gone for all those years. They may have still seemed like just any neighbors, reminding Tess that while so much of her memory revolved around this town, it had gone on without her. Anyway, he cut them a chunk of cheddar off the block and fished pickles from the jar. He got a loaf of bakery bread off the cooling rack and sliced bologna so thin you could read through it.

As they turned to leave, Tess heard Jamie say, "Oh, crap." He steered her to the back of the store, behind a rack of potato chips. "I think that damned *People* reporter is out there using the phone," he whispered.

Bells tinkled as the front door opened. Jamie actually knelt down and studied the CheeTos on the bottom rack. And it made giggles bubble up in Tess even as she heard Heather ask for directions to the church parsonage.

And then the bells jingled again. Heather was gone. Tess let the giggles loose. Jamie caught them, and they crouched by the chips holding each other and laughing breathlessly until they noticed Old Man Kimball standing over them, quizzing them with a stern look.

Afterward, the tension that had built between them all morning seemed cleared. It felt like the morning after a thunderstorm. Tess teased Jamie about Heather prowling after him, and he took back roads, heading south out of town to the Jenkins farm. "She's not entirely harmless," Tess said. "She did get this far."

"Today," he said, "I'm incognito." He winked and tipped his hat lower over one eye.

"Then you better keep your butt in this truck," she tweaked him. "Because there are women all over these hills wearing T-shirts of your Wrangler's. Might as well be a Wanted poster."

He laughed sheepishly, truly embarrassed, and pulled in at a white farmhouse. A dog nipped at the tires in greeting, his tail windmilling. "Let me do it," Jamie said.

He got out and knelt to pet the collie. Paul Jenkins opened the screen door, a feeble man in patched overalls. "Y-ello," he called.

"Hey," Jamie answered, walking toward the porch as the dog bounded around him. Tess could hear nothing but the murmur of their conversation, but she saw Jamie reach for the man's gnarled hand. Mr. Jenkins leaned against the door frame, Jamie against a column on the porch. Laughter carried to her once or twice. The old farmer was talking his leg off. She saw Jamie shift positions, signaling he was about to leave. But then he would stay a bit longer, shift again. She sat there smiling, the breeze moving slow as smoke through the car, and she wished she could paint that picture, the way the two looked on the porch, the way some things are timeless.

Jamie slipped finally into the pickup and echoed her impressions. "Well, nothing's changed."

"He remembered you?"

"Let's say he remembered me as if I were here yesterday and all the years I was away didn't even exist."

"People are sweeter here, aren't they?" she said, mildly amazed after her years in the city where people were nice in a way that outsiders couldn't even distinguish.

Jamie laughed sort of apologetically. "Actually," he said, "I think he's kind of lost it. He's kind of living in the past. He told me to keep myself out of trouble. The Calhouns think every hair on my head is gold, is how he put it."

"Oh," she said almost mournfully. "The whole town seems like that. Old, older, oldest."

Jamie pulled off the road and onto the rutted grass leading to a gate in the fence around Jenkins's pasture. Tess jumped out and unlatched the barbed-wire gate, which was only fastened with a loop of wire over the nearest fence post. She dragged it open, ushering Jamie through with an elaborate gesture of welcome. His laughter trailed out of the car as he nosed the car through. As kids, they had been given full run of the place because Jamie helped Paul Jenkins haul hay every hot August when the insects hissed like new fire and the dust rose like smoke behind the pickup truck that inched through the fields followed by men bending their backs to the bales and hoisting them up. As an added benefit, the farmer had offered Jamie a swim in his twisting strand of Sugar Creek whenever he wanted it. Evidently, the offer still stood. Jamie followed the twin dirt ruts that headed through the pasture and down to the creek. As the pickup crept by it, a little holstein calf arched its tail and capered away on its knobby legs. Its mama and a dozen other cows didn't stir except to follow the Ford with their gaze. Tails switched away flies. Mouths chewed old cud.

The fields were new growth and looked as cropped as a lawn in town. Spring was chartreuse gauze in the willows that fringed the creek. Tess breathed deeply, luxuriating, as she stepped out of the truck and onto the grassy bank where Jamie had first put into words his love for her. The creek was running clear over the amber rocks and then deepening to green over the swimming hole. There was still a gray knotted rope hanging from the old oak, which stood with its catacomb of roots exposed by seasons of rushing water.

"If we could just get you into some cutoffs, nothing would be different," Jamie said, slipping his arms around her and holding her against his chest. "Gets my blood up just being here," he whispered into her hair.

She laughed with abandon, remembering how many times they had slipped off down here to find their way slowly into the deepest parts of each other. Her laughter bubbled up out of her like the fresh, cold spring that fed into this very creek. It tickled her so much that she kept laughing. She was among friends—the oak and the sycamores and willows, all of which had witnessed that first night under the stars. The trees had kept quiet about all those nights that followed, nights when the two of them had come down here to touch and awaken sensations that demanded more touching and more. She laughed. Jamie was here, and the birds were singing springtime, and they had all been here before. "I love you," she said, turning to embrace Jamie so hard that his back made a little popping sound.

He laughed and kissed her. They walked hand in hand down to the rushing brook. She knelt and dipped her hand in it, brought a cool splash of it to her face. Soon, they had their jeans rolled up and were wading around in the current, competing to catch crawdads and bigger crawdads and one-clawed crawdads. They looked for tadpoles in the muddy pocket where part of the flow got diverted and came to a still stop and where they had once long ago seen a little frog treading water in the sun, looking like he could not be happier anywhere.

"Are you hungry yet?" she asked him, because he always was.

"For one thing," he said, looking at her lustily.

She giggled and said, "Jamie, it's broad daylight. Just imagine." She meant imagine what would happen if someone chanced upon them— Tess Boone and Buck Campbell—cavorting on the banks of Sugar Creek. He chose to imagine another scenario: "I am," he said. "I am."

She led him up the knoll to the cool grass by the car. She got out the impromptu picnic, and he opened the truck doors and pushed in a tape of Lyle Lovett, who sang "This Old Porch" as they sprawled on the grass eating cheese and bread and drinking Coke cold out of the creek.

"This is the life," he said as he stretched out and laid his head on the pillow of her lap. Tess put her hand in his hair. "It might have been," she said.

Together, they absorbed the balm of the sunshine, each caught up in thoughts of what might have been.

"But it wouldn't have been this life, would it?" he asked. "It wouldn't have been like this?"

"No," she said, then added: "Not if you believe Pop anyway."

"I would've had to drink a lot of beer to ignore what I was doing to you," Jamie said. "But, on the upside, I would've had a gut I could rest my beer on while I was watching *America's Funniest Home Videos.*"

"I would've loved your gut," she said, patting him on the patch of hair low on his taut stomach. He spent a lot of time in the gym. She could tell. Free weights and Versiclimber, probably.

"And I would've loved the way you looked pregnant. All round," he said. He was wistful again. "But you weren't made for that, Tessie. Your dad had you thinking big thoughts. And it was no more than you deserved. You've got a mind. I remember sitting in the gym, the day you graduated, and you were standing up there giving that speech and talking about wishing for wings. And I knew you were gonna fly, knew it then for sure. I knew I was gonna have to scramble to hang on to you. I thought I could. I knew I had to. I thought we could find our way to a place where we could both be happy."

She sighed. As far as she knew, that place was only the space stretched between them now, only these stolen hours.

"Are you?" she asked. "Happy?"

"At this moment, right here, right now. Yes."

He reached up and pulled her earlobe. "But in Nashville, on the road. No. Happy is not the word for what I am. I belong to other people, not myself. People read articles, and they think they know me. They make me cookies, send me flowers. Once, this woman made me an afghan. Do you know how many hours goes into knitting one of those things? It makes me feel like the hindquarters of despicable to know that my chauffeur lets his dog sleep on it."

He shook his head. "Buck Campbell is a royal pain in the arse."

She laughed sympathetically, and he went on: "There's just always something aching in me, wanting more. I feel guilty about that, having so much and only wanting more. I have someone who drives me everywhere, another one who squeezes me juice every morning, another one who rubs my feet and my back. I mean, *every* time I go into my bathroom, somebody has folded my damn toilet paper into a little point."

The look of undiluted disdain that pulled his brow low over his eyes made her giggle. "I know," she said. "I hear myself complain. And I think, I've got a job that pays more money than ever ran through Pop's hands. I fly a hundred thousand miles a year. But deep down most of the time, I'm something close to miserable."

Jamie kissed the crease of skin between her thumb and forefinger.

"Why is one way of life so far from the other?" she asked, not in a manner that said she expected an answer from him or from anyone else ever. "I mean, why can't I be *successful* . . ." She said the word disdainfully, though she had sacrificed everything, sacrificed *him*, for success. "Why can't I have some of that and some of this? Why does the fact that I wanted to write, why does that mean that I couldn't have you lying in my lap all the time, looking up at me with those eyes?"

Her voice rose up on a peak, trembled there. When she spoke again, it was as though she were abandoning herself to a slide down the other side of the slope, relinquishing herself. She answered her own questions, with resentment seeping up around her words: "It's because we had to make all the hardest decisions when we were kids. And what kids. I mean, we were desperate. I was. I saw Pop scraping all the time, and Mama with that tight mouth of hers all stitched up so she could suck on her bitterness. I bought the dream. I bought the escape. But I was too stupid to know that it wasn't *all* worth escaping. Some of it I needed. Some of it was the best I was ever gonna get."

They were quiet for some time as the sun splintered through the trees and fell in shifting shards on them and the new grass where they sat. The creek gurgled to itself through the shallows and then hushed as it ran through the swimming hole. In the trees, the birds chattered. A cow's lowing carried across the pasture.

"I daydream about you sometimes," he said. "When it's bad."

"Like what?"

"Sometimes I dream that we're right here and you look just the way you look now, with all those flames flickerin' up in your hair 'cause of the sun. And those green eyes. I always think about our kids. Two of 'em, playing down in that creek and running up here to show us their crawdaddies.

109

You know, kids that never need Band-Aids, kids that are never sad enough to sing themselves to sleep because they're just daydream kids."

"You're lucky to have even that kind, the daydream kind," she began. "And don't be hurt by this. But I don't let myself think about it. I never have. At first, the guilt would have just washed me under. And then I guess it would just have been too painful to flirt with what might have been."

She thought to herself that it is possible to fly too high. You can fly so high that you can't even see the real things down below, so high you can't see the signposts that get you where you want to go. All she said to him was: "I've got too much and not anywhere near enough."

"I know, baby," he said, pulling her down into the grass with him. "I know."

CHAPTER FIFTEEN

"Tell me," he said later as they were tenderfoot wading in the creek. "Tell me about your life now. What it's like. So I can picture you wherever I am."

"Don't make me think about it now," she said, kicking a spray of water at him. "It's another lifetime. And this one is so short."

Jamie splashed her back, blew her a kiss.

They ambled arm in arm along the banks of the creek, winding with it for miles, crawling under fences and passing cows who looked up at them with placid eyes. If they talked, it was about yesterday, the past that seemed like yesterday. They didn't mention tomorrow, only held hands and walked through the springtime as though it would last forever.

Up the hill, they found the old Robb place, the rock cottage he had pictured them in. Lilacs still bloomed, and irises. But weeds were doing their work of obliteration. They sat on the steps in the sun. There were new little flowers, tiny as baby's buttons, in the grass, and bright forget-me-nots growing loose. He picked a sprig, and held it out to her.

"Forget-me-not," she said wistfully.

"Never have."

"It's the flower," she told him.

"I know."

She kissed him, and he whispered, "I always felt you tugging at me, like the ocean feels the moon."

By then, the light was aging to a golden glow, and the wind was picking up from the south. And when they finally wound back to the truck, the sun was setting behind storm clouds. Tess stood and watched it, watched the gilt edge of the storm flame, watched the sky throb like an ember. "I've missed too many sunsets," she said. "You can't see them in the city."

"Well, then," Jamie told her, "we'd better make the most of this one." He hooked her around her narrow waist and two-stepped on the banks of Sugar Creek, then slowed to a waltz and finally to one of those tight little revolutions they used to dance in the high school gymnasium when it was hung with crepe paper and balloons. They held fast and moved so that the whole world spun around them. The sky turned violet, then purple, then electric blue.

He began to sing as they revolved together. It happened so naturally and built so gradually from the inner hum of him that it seemed as though the song had always been there, coursing through them. He sang a song full of longing and tenderness, and Tess clung to him, to the shivering effervescence of his song against her body. She did not so much listen to the words as she entered the song or let it enter her. Before they had ever loved each other completely, all the way, this had been their lovemaking. When they were still too shy or too scared to reveal themselves fully to one another, they had encompassed their desire in an embrace, letting his song race along the nerves that seemed to run in unbroken strands from her body to his.

Jamie had admitted once that he started singing when his mama left. He would sing himself to sleep. It was better than crying. The Calhouns would walk toward his door to listen, and he would hush, ashamed. But when they would walk away, go off to bed, he would sing again, songs that his mama had sung. Tess used to picture him, a tiny blond boy tucked in, singing "Mama, Don't Let Your Babies Grow Up to Be Cowboys." Later, he started in on songs that he heard in church with the Calhouns. He loved "Amazing Grace." He never sang for anybody else but Tess, not openly anyway. But it was just natural that music would bubble up from inside him when he was with her, because that's when the longing in him got too much. As a boy, he had longed for his mama, and so he sang. As a young man, he longed to be with Tess and couldn't, not yet, not fully, and so he sang to soothe them both.

Now, older and too wise to the way the world could and would pry them apart, they danced in the purple dusk until they could hear the thunder throbbing closer, until they couldn't ignore the lightning pulsing in the clouds like a heartbeat. After they got into the truck and pulled back across the field and out onto the road, the first dagger of lightning broke free from the sky and stitched a crooked way to the ground. She shivered and moved closer to him, even across the gearshift and console. He gathered her in. "C'mere," he said.

The windshield wipers beat with their two hearts.

CHAPTER SIXTEEN

The rain was ricocheting hard off the windshield when Jamie nosed the truck up beside the little log cottage in the clearing. Years seemed to have passed since they left that morning. The drive back itself had started light and then grown heavy with the silent acknowledgment that what waited for them was only reality.

"You can't see the stars when it rains," she said, hating herself for feeling fragile now that they were back in the part of the universe where they could be found.

"Tonight we don't need the stars," he said. "We've got each other."

"But . . ."

"Georgia went on down to Nashville. She'll stall everyone for another day," he said. "We've got tonight."

Tonight stood between them and the rest of their lives. Tomorrow he would go back to his obligations; she to hers. At a certain point, life became not just the promises you made but the contracts you signed. You assigned yourself an orbit, and barring a collapse of the solar system, you stayed in it. Tess had launched herself into hers long ago, and Buck Campbell had become a force stronger than even Jamie could control. He was at the center of a network of recording deals, concert schedules, television appearances. Livelihoods were founded on him. And so they had tonight.

They ran holding hands up onto the porch and into the cabin, closing the door on that thought—*only tonight*—as though it were a wolf pacing around their walls. Inside, the phone was ringing. Jamie ignored it, toweling the raindrops off her hair, and then kneeling before the hearth to light a fire. Tess set out the Big Macs and fries they had picked up. Soon, the fire crackled orange, ranging high and roaring. Then it settled and blue flames swam, hissing over the logs. They reclined on woven pillows before it and ate the food as though it were from Lutece and not McDonald's.

"Happiness makes you hungry," he observed, kissing her. She giggled and fed him another French fry. The phone began to ring again.

"Aren't you gonna get that?" she asked, after somebody had hung up and then called back three times. The phone had become like some approaching storm, thundering ominously in the distance, and Tess was worn down to just wanting the lightning to strike, the gales to whip, the clouds to move over and past and be gone.

Jamie just shook his head.

Exasperation overwhelmed Tess. "I feel like she's right here in this room with us."

Jamie ate three fries at once and said blandly, "She's not."

Tess felt her emotion flare, heard it in her own voice. "Yes, she is. Because you won't just tell me about her. About you. About the two of you."

His answer was mild, but stunned her to the spine. "It's none of your business."

For several minutes she couldn't move, couldn't speak. When she could, she said quietly, "Why are you being this way to me?"

He shrugged. "Why don't you stop asking so many questions, Tess? Your tape recorder isn't running, right? I don't see any notepad."

"I just thought we were part of each other's lives." She was nearly pleading for mercy.

But he didn't give it. "You left me, remember?"

The phone began to ring again. He got up, yanked the cord out of the wall, and went out onto the porch. After a minute, she followed, and found him staring off into the rain, his shoulders sagging.

She touched his arm and said, "I had to."

He looked at her with harsh disbelief widening his eyes. "You really still believe that, don't you?"

She nodded. "Who I was then, what I knew . . ."

"What you knew was what your old man told you."

"He loved me," she said.

"I loved you."

"Then you shouldn't have just let it happen. You shouldn't have run away. The road goes both ways, Jamie." She was right about this and suddenly knew it. He didn't have to walk out of her life just because she told him to.

"Do you want to know where the road goes, Tess? Do you?"

"To Georgia." The spite in her voice surprised even her.

"By way of hell."

Tess turned and went to the porch swing, sat down, folded her arms around her stomach, held herself. "I've asked," she said.

"Yeah, and every time you ask, I feel like it's Tess Boone, bloodless celebrity reporter."

She couldn't lift her eyes to meet his gaze. Her answer sounded spindly. "You know me better than that."

"Do I?" he asked, coming to sit next to her.

Her voice cracked. "You did."

"I trusted my Tess with everything, the whole shebang. And it didn't matter, because she still left." He swung back and forth, the cool wet air rushing over them, between them.

"I'm sorry," she said, and the quality of her voice must have told him the words had deep roots in her heart.

He softened. "I'm sorry, too. Sorry because I thought I was home at last when I found you. Sorry because all these years have been wasted, thrown away. And especially sorry because I'm married to a good woman who deserves my love—only I will never have that to give her. Because I'm in love with you." He picked up her hand, kissed her across the knuckles.

"Why?"

He grinned, "Why am I in love with you?"

She shook her head. "Why did you marry her?"

The chain on the porch swing creaked with each push of his legs, and finally he spoke, "Because she did save me—more than once."

"From 'drinking and fighting and goin' around with the wrong women.'" She scratched quotation marks in the air as she used Georgia's words.

"Well, that's her version. It was more saving me from myself. I was hurting after you. And if it hadn't been for her, I might never have gotten on a stage or shaken hands with a record exec. . . ."

"So pay her a percentage, but . . ." Tess could feel herself losing it.

"I owe her more than that." Jamie looked at Tess, scrutinized her, then sighed. "She was in business with a guy who liked to gamble and then accuse her of losing money running the club. Turned out, he also liked to beat the crap out of her. And I caught him at it one night, plowing into her full out. There was blood running all over her, and I just lost it."

He sat looking at his hands as though they had betrayed him, and Tess thought of his mother, of the blood coursing down her face like tears. He had always been the steadiest of men, had the mildest of tempers. He was gentle above all else. She could see how fresh his sense of shame still was.

Jamie continued. "Afterward, the guy was in pretty rough shape. And, Georgia, she sat right there by his hospital bed until he woke up—so she could make sure he'd tell the cops a different story. Which he did, and which he still does to people like you."

It was all clear to Tess now. "So she paid him off and blackmailed you into marrying her." She couldn't disguise the twisted sense of triumph she felt.

Jamie looked at her with something near disgust. "See, there it is," he spit.

"There what is?"

"That bloodless tabloid thing."

She looked at the hands in her lap, saw the fingernails as though they weren't her own, but some stranger's.

He went on. "I mean, you of all people must know that there can be more between a man and a woman than animal lust or, or blackmail."

"Maybe I just wanted it to be nothing more than blackmail," she said quietly. She swung her eyes to his and saw that he understood, that he could forgive her that emotion.

"Does she know? About us?"

"Enough."

"Does she care?"

"I do. She doesn't deserve this."

Tess got up and walked to the porch railing, wished for the rain to wash away the pain. "None of us deserves this," she told him.

He took her in his arms and kissed her then, long and tenderly. Then he lifted her, carried her inside, and settled her by the fire.

He stretched out alongside her, and for what seemed like some version of eternity, they kissed, pausing occasionally to hold one another in the stillness. Tess's mind was not still, at first, stirred up by his secrets. But his tenderness soon began to seep in and to muffle the clamor. She began to feel peaceful, sheltered from the phantom of that other life. He kissed her forehead and her cheekbones, ran his lips along the cup of her ear and to the delicate concavity just behind it. He moved gingerly down her neck and into the hollow of her breastbone, his breath blowing like a warm summer night across her skin.

He lifted her then and carried her to the bed. He undressed her slowly: pulling away the sweater, pressing his lips against the skin where the lace of her bra strap had etched its pattern. And then she sat on the bed, shivering in the force of their desire, and watched as he stripped off his shirt and his jeans. She reached up to him and pulled him down with her until they were stretched full together. She could feel the silk and fur of him. Their skin rustled like finely woven fabric, and their bodies knitted themselves into the rhythm that they had known, had not forgotten from those far-off days on the grassy knoll by the creek when the stars had sizzled in the night sky and the wind had set the trees to whispering. Then, Jamie had ached toward her and she toward him until there was no power anywhere that could move them in any other direction, until they could only meld in a sweet rush of sensation that obliterated all the world, all words, all thought, until he was inside her and she in him, and they were all. It happened on those starry nights, and it happened now as the rain played music they ceased to hear.

CHAPTER SEVENTEEN

Tess woke up with his arms around her, with the scent of him rising like mist from the sheets, and she realized that these past nights had been the first time in all their loving that they had ever shared a bed. Often, she had woken like this with other men; their arms around her had always felt like shackles. Never had she woken eager to see the day with the man beside her. She had wanted him to get up and get dressed and go, just go. Not that she hadn't spent occasional mornings with one of them, eating pumpkin muffins and drinking champagne cocktails and discussing the *Book Review.* She had just always felt panic coursing up inside her, poisoning her.

What cruel irony. Jamie would wake soon. He would get up, get dressed, and go, just go. And she had ordained it when she was eighteen years old and more powerful than she even guessed. She had done it to herself.

She lay still, not wanting him to mount back into consciousness, wanting more time to memorize the way his chest brushed her back with his every breath, the way his calf curved against hers, the way his hand held her just below the rib cage. Tess did not want to forget how Jamie smelled, felt, tasted. Not this time. Not again.

All these years, he had haunted her, though she could not recognize the apparition's face. He haunted her through the stars and through the music on the radio. He held her so steadfastly in his thrall that she could not accept any other embrace, could not find any other man worthy. Jamie had been with her all these years, and he would be still when this morning ended. What they shared stretched between them over all distance. It shaped their every movement, ached inside them even when they called it by another name. Sometimes they called it loneliness, sometimes restlessness. Sometimes they called it the blues. But it was always the one calling the other's name across time and miles and every obstacle, like the moon calling the tides forth on the ocean. They could not be apart, not truly, not ever.

Outside, a mourning dove called its longing through the pines to its lover.

Jamie stirred. He pulled her close against him, kissed her neck.

CHAPTER EIGHTEEN

On the flight back to New York, Tess didn't look out the window as the plane raced along the runway and lifted itself over the green farmland; she didn't watch as she left home again. She felt as though she were traveling in a bubble of loss through which nothing could reach her, bringing comfort or pain.

Logan greeted her at the office the next day with a steaming bowl of *cafe au lait*, chocolate grated on top. He complimented the color in her cheeks, the cut of her skirt. "Nice fabric," he said, rubbing it between his fingers. "It falls so beautifully." She finally told him to stop squirming.

"So you've forgiven me?" he asked sheepishly.

"Never," she said.

And then he told her that she was on the schedule for back-to-back covers. The only thing was, the Triumvirate couldn't decide if they wanted Sam Conrad first or if they wanted Buck Campbell. So she should do both first, Logan said, smirking apologetically at the conundrum.

She asked how much time, and he quailed dramatically and said a week. And she just turned to the Macintosh and double-clicked on a file.

"What was Buck like after you got to know him?" Logan asked. It was the part he loved best, dishing the good stuff before anybody else could, before she put it into print.

She didn't answer.

"Did you peel off his secrets until he was standing there naked?" he pried playfully.

She started typing.

"Tess?"

The keyboard clattered under her fingers. Giving up, he kissed her on the top of the head and left her to her stories. She transcribed her Conrad story the first day, did a draft the second, zipped it to Logan's computer. He E-mailed back his enthusiasm: "Loved that left-buttock quote!!!" he wrote. Then one by one the editors E-mailed their respective hats-offs. Reading them gave Tess something to do as she sat looking at her computer screen. She couldn't transcribe her notes for Buck Campbell, couldn't stand to hear Georgia's lies, couldn't bear to hear Jamie's voice disguised under the star's persona.

She procrastinated by turning on her office

television set, flying through the channels until she was ambushed by Mary Hart chirping about Buck Campbell in Tokyo. The crowd shots showed thousands of young people in faded jeans and cowboy boots, stomping and carrying on in a most western fashion. She didn't notice Logan come up and stand behind her until he whistled at a clip of Buck on stage. The footage cut to Georgia and Buck in a crowd of kids. Tess zapped it. The television crackled off.

"Do you have an ETA on your piece?" Logan asked. She just looked up at him and mouthed the word "no."

After he left, she stared out her window. Jamie had told her that the first time they parted, it had been like stopping running water—unbelievable that something so vital and strong could suddenly cease to be. And of course their love hadn't ended but had instead gone underground to somehow flow and nourish them even as they were unaware. And now it was like trying to stop running water again, although it wasn't being diverted this time. Her emotion ran all through her, overwhelmed her. She was drowning in Jamie.

Tess tried to write her story, tried distancing Jamie by concentrating only on Buck Campbell. But the writing was as difficult as the interview had been. She paced with coffee that grew cold before she drank it. She closed her office door. She wrote at home in her nightgown until late at night and then got dressed and went for a walk along Broadway. She sat at her PowerBook, finally strapping on the transcribing headphones, and making herself play his voice over and over, punctuated with Georgia's—the dream and the reality lashing her like wind. She tried to capture Buck Campbell, but Georgia obscured him. A story about Buck Campbell was really a story about Georgia. He was her invention, the Frankenstein creation who had turned on her with emotions more real than she had wanted to imagine him having. But of course, Tess couldn't write that. And try as she might, she could not bring the star to life on paper as Georgia had brought him to life on stage. Buck Campbell belonged to the other woman. Tess had a penetrating style, and with Buck there was nothing below the surface—except Jamie.

She was typing nonsensically, trying to jump-start herself, when the phone rang in her office. It was Heather Trace. Tess turned to look out the window as she listened. Heather told her she was doing a cover story on Buck Campbell. Tess congratulated her. The other woman hesitated.

Tess preempted, "How's Jack?"

Heather missed a beat, and Tess could almost hear her thinking. "Jack?" she asked finally.

"Your editor," Tess reminded her. "Tall guy, wife, three point five kids."

"He's fine," Heather said brusquely, recovering and parrying: "Look, I have some questions for you about Buck Campbell."

"I don't think that's appropriate."

"Well, I'm sending over a picture you might want to comment on," Heather said in a voice that Tess recognized as artificially confident. The fax machine was already pressing out an image as Heather explained about having lucked into sitting next to someone at the Wayne Newton concert from Prosperity, someone who knew Buck Campbell as Jamie, who knew Tess too.

The fax was spattered and dark, but Tess could make it out.

"Not interested," Tess told Heather as her other phone line began buzzing for her attention.

"I have questions," Heather persisted.

"My other line's ringing," Tess said, punching a button to disconnect Heather.

She uncurled the fax machine's crude black-and-white image: Jamie held her in his arms, kissing her. The creek ran obscurely behind them. That damn photographer must have used a lens as long as his arm, Tess thought.

The phone buzzed at her again.

"Hello," she muttered, feeling so far away that no voice could draw her back from the moment of their embrace and from the collision with the realization that it had been desecrated.

And then she heard, "This is Georgia Hill."

CHAPTER NINETEEN

Tess grabbed a yellow cab to La Guardia. She usually called a sleek, comfortable company car to cut through all the traffic and out to the airport. But she couldn't even settle in her chair long enough to phone one, then wait on hold for them to give her a number, then wait again for the car to show up under the flags outside the building.

Logan had tried to stop her in the hallway, wanting to know about her Buck Campbell cover, but she had brushed past him, and hurt, he had called after her, "The sharks are circling."

Little does he know, she thought as the cab

jolted crazily over every pothole between midtown Manhattan and Queens. Fortunately, there was little traffic, and the Egyptian cabbie had no compunction against veering between lanes at ninety miles per hour. He sang with Whitney Houston at the top of his lungs.

Once at the airport, Tess went to a security office and explained herself. A guard led her down long corridors with no windows. She thought they must be underground, and she lost all sense of direction. But as her steps fell ringingly on the linoleum tiles, she began to find her bearings. A certain professional calm took over, and by the time she was riding across the tarmac, she felt strong. She felt in control.

His private plane was long and gray and discreet. She had seen it rise into the air at the Ozark airport, had seen its goose-like profile, neck stretched into another time, another place, away. She had seen it taking him away.

A young man met her at the bottom of the stairs, directed her to go up them. Georgia was waiting just inside, talking on a phone. She didn't look at Tess but pointed at some southwestern-style sofas where she should sit. The faxed picture of Tess and Jamie—fuzzy but clear enough to tell the story—was lying on a coffee table.

Speaking into the receiver, Georgia said, "See that you do." Her tone was clipped. "Don't bother him with it. Just see that it's done. I don't want him to worry. It will affect his voice." She hung up, walked back toward Tess, sat down across from her.

"She faxed me some pictures," Georgia said to Tess.

"I'm sorry she did that," Tess answered. She noticed how thin her own voice was.

Georgia looked at her for the first time but couldn't hold her gaze steady. "Buck told me everything," she said, studying her own hands. She held one palm against the other, the fingers opening and closing around each other. They were shaking. Tess noticed the gold band on her wedding finger and tried to think of something to say, but failed.

"Do you love him?" Georgia said, her voice directed more at her own hands than at Tess.

"Yes," Tess said. "I've loved him as long as I can remember. I'm sorry."

"Don't be," Georgia said too quickly. "I gave up on love, the way you mean it, a long time ago. Buck and I have always been honest with each other, always cared for each other. I knew there was something, or someone, that he was never going to get over. He knew that I was devoted to him, to what he could do with himself. I never had any expectations. It was just easier to marry, to fence out the rest of the world. Everybody wanted a piece of him, so many fans, opportunists . . ."

Even as Georgia said the words, her face betrayed her, emotion crossing it the way weather patterns cross the open sky out West. *She loves him,* Tess thought. *She always hoped someday— if she took the right care of him—he would love her back the same way.* But nothing came to Tess that she could possibly say aloud, that she could use as a bridge between them.

"He wanted to walk away from everything. Wanted you." Georgia looked up and into her eyes. "And I couldn't let him do it. He has obliga-

127

tions. He's a corporation. Too many things, too many people, depend on him."

Tess hadn't known. She and Jamie had just said goodbye, no promises. Just goodbye. So now to hide her surprise, to just say something, anything, she blurted: "I can imagine."

"No, you can't," Georgia said. "Not unless you've held it together the way I have. Year after year. Day after day. I hold it together, and people talk behind my back how I'm a controlling bitch, running his life, when all I'm trying to do is not let what he has go to waste. He has such a beautiful gift."

Tess was silent. She couldn't imagine.

Georgia picked up the fax, looked at it. Tess flinched, felt exposed, felt ashamed at having betrayed this woman who had been betrayed too many times by life itself.

"You know her?" Georgia asked.

"You mean Heather?"

Georgia nodded.

"I taught her the ropes," Tess said.

"Well, she's about to hang him with them."

Tess felt her professional spine straighten. "It's not the end of the world," she said mildly. "Celebrities have affairs all the time, don't they?"

"Buck Campbell doesn't. He's the Tom Hanks, the Jimmy Stewart, of country music. He's one of the good guys."

Tess looked at her hands. Her knuckles were going white. *His image?* she thought. *This is about his blasted image?*

Georgia spoke more quietly. "She's got reporters in Nashville, swarming my former partner and some people who used to take care of him . . . a woman who knows everything, who's very righteous about it."

Clearly, Georgia had been paying her ex-partner to keep quiet. And, Tess knew that if Heather dug up this part of the story, it would hurt Jamie more than it hurt Buck Campbell. Jamie was ashamed of having done lasting harm, even to someone so vile. He had been young, and his past had reared up to avenge the blood of a defenseless woman, of his mother somehow. That was defensible. But to have taken it so far and to have allowed Georgia to bury it under his money . . .

Georgia's voice was muted with panic. "Look, I hate asking for help . . . I've always known that if I wanted anything done, I had to do it myself."

Tess saw that Georgia's lips were quivering and that she was pressing them together, fighting for control over herself. Georgia saw herself losing what she had wholly invested herself in: her career, her marriage, even herself, because who was she if she couldn't do everything for him? Old regret rose up in Tess. She thought of the work on her mother's hands, the endless effort, the hopelessness.

"I'm only asking for Buck . . ." Georgia managed to say.

Before she spoke, Tess looked at Georgia long enough to make the other woman meet her eyes. Her voice was solid: "Buck Campbell doesn't mean anything to me. Just Jamie . . ."

"You should know . . . Buck Campbell is all I care about," Georgia replied softly.

Each read the meaning in the other's eyes.

CHAPTER TWENTY

Tess worked fast. She didn't let herself think too much about what she was doing. She held Jamie up front in her mind. She didn't look past him. She went back to the office and up to the thirtieth floor, dropped in on her friend Jill, who worked on the financial side of the magazine.

"How's the rock?" Tess asked, and Jill waved her huge diamond engagement ring around so that it sparked wildly.

Tess clucked appreciatively. Jill's handsome Italian boyfriend had proposed on the top of the Empire State Building, and she and Tess had lunched at Sign of the Dove in celebration. They drank champagne and ate raspberries with cream. It was rare that colleagues from the editorial and the business side of the magazine socialized. But Jill and Tess had a similar sense of fun—and a secret.

"Remember that little game of Tryst you played with the expense reports?" Tess asked with a sly smile.

"You mean the one where he works late; she works late. He takes a late-night hotel room; she turns in a receipt for the restaurant in the lobby for the same night. And the next morning they have two cabs with identical distance and time charges within two minutes of each other." Jill grinned at her. "That one?"

"Would you trust me with a copy of it?"

"Hon, I'd trust you with the rock itself if you asked for it."

Next, Tess tracked down Jimmy in the mail room. He was a lanky dreamer who rode motorcycles and read war books and was tight with the security guards in the lobby. He didn't quite fit into the cosmopolitan atmosphere of the office, and Tess adored him for it. Jimmy had once offered to stand sentinel at her door against a perverted rock star she had interviewed who sent flowers every day with huge suggestive pistils and explicit handwritten notes. Jimmy had told her then that he had once taken a bullet for someone, and he was willing to do it for her.

"Hey, Jimbo," she said, finding him bent over a review copy of a Patton biography that she had loaned him. "Remember that security photo the guards showed you and you showed me?"

"No amount of weed is gonna erase *that* memory, Tess."

She laughed. "Do you think you could get a copy of it for me? Just for a little while?"

"Sure," he said, unlocking a drawer underneath the cabinet where extra pens and notepads were kept. He pulled the photograph out of a stack of girlie poses that she had seen him and the messengers ogle when it was late in the day and nobody needed much.

"You kept it?" she blurted.

"Sure," he shrugged.

She told Heather to meet her at Starbucks. Heather got there first, and she looked edgy when Tess walked in. Tess thought that Heather must already have her finger on the trigger so she would have the courage to go through with this.

131

Tess sat down across from her.

"Don't you want to get a coffee?" Heather asked. "Their mochaccinos are *made* for you, real chocolatey."

"Not in the mood." Tess held her in a steady gaze.

Heather looked down at her coffee, swirled it, tried a friendly tack: "You must be really proud of him . . ."

Tess didn't blink.

". . . of Buck. Or Jamie . . ." Heather said tentatively, her eyes grazing Tess's. The *People* reporter fiddled with the spoon next to her coffee as she stammered on. "But I'm not getting the whole picture. I mean, if he loves *you*, why is he still with her?"

Tess didn't respond.

"And I thought, it might work out for you . . . with him . . . if you could help me with the puzzle."

"Oh, you're doing this for *me?*" Tess snorted out her incredulity, her disdain.

Heather looked up at her with eyes that practically implored her to buy it, to go with this line.

Tess went on. "That's why you tracked me like an animal and sent me those pictures. Because you want to help me?"

"It's my job."

"I know what your job is, and this isn't it."

"I'm not doing anything you haven't done."

"Wrong," Tess flared. "I've never done a journalistic ambush. I write stories about people who invite me into their lives because I'm a beneficial parasite. They let me extract a few juicy things; I give them hype on the cover of a major magazine. I get an invitation to suck blood, or, honey, I don't suck."

"What kind of a journalist is that?"

"A *celebrity* journalist. Don't take yourself so seriously. You're not Woodward and Bernstein. And Buck Campbell sure isn't Nixon. Face it, Heather, we do stories about people who get their power from boob jobs and press agents, and from some talent for entertaining that lets people with hard lives kick back and enjoy themselves."

"Buck Campbell is a public person," Heather countered.

"He's still entitled to a private life. Nobody elected him."

Heather looked around as if for reinforcements and then set her jaw in defiance. "I'm going to Nashville in the morning. Our stringer has found a woman who worked for Georgia Hill's ex-partner."

"Don't do this . . ." Tess began.

Heather pressed: "You can help me or not."

". . . because I don't want to have to do *this*." Tess pulled a bulky envelope out of her backpack and pushed it across the table to Heather.

She felt a queasiness in the pit of her stomach as she watched Heather fumble to open it, as she watched Heather see the his-and-her expense accounts and then the photo taken by an automatic security camera. Heather stared at the image. She stared at evidence that she had compromised herself with Jack Bates on the couch by the elevator waiting room at the magazine.

"You're not going to show these to anybody, are you?" The color had completely leached out of her face.

"No," Tess said. "And I didn't show them to anybody the first time somebody showed them to me. And I didn't tell anybody. I *tried* to tell you to slow down, not take so many shortcuts, remember?"

Tess had taken Heather to lunch, tried to counsel her without embarrassing her. At the time, Heather had been a promising editorial assistant. Tess had always made sure through Logan that Heather got to do some reporting and sidebar pieces. But, when Tess had found out what was going on with Heather and Jack Bates and had tried to tell her that careers take time, Heather had seemed to think it was just an attempt to undermine her. She had thought Tess was threatened by her up-and-coming potential. Soon after, Jack had taken over the editorship of *People* magazine. He had recruited Heather, and she had gone. And now she was behind the wheel of a promotion that had a powerful engine she was unprepared to control.

"You're young," Tess told her now. "But someday you're going to know for sure that we all live in glass houses, and we'd all be better off not to sling around so many stones."

Heather stood up, looking fierce. She didn't say a word as she packed up her notebook and her tape recorder. Tess thought there might be tears behind the ferocity, but the young woman disappeared out the door before revealing herself in any way.

Tess ordered a mochaccino and a chocolate bar with cherries. As she watched people parade by on the street, she thought what she had thought so many times, that power corrupts, celebrity corrodes. It's just adoration, fans lapping like ocean swells at the edge of the stage. But even water wears away at things, wears away at the hardest stone until there's a crumbling cliff. And anybody who comes too close can lose their footing, plunge off the edge, get torn apart by the crashing waves. Tess had always thought she wouldn't venture that near. And she wouldn't have, not for anyone else. Not for anyone but him.

CHAPTER TWENTY-ONE

Back at the office the next morning, she had given up staring at the faint throbbing of her computer screen and instead was watching out the window as boats trailed like slugs through the Hudson. She was still, more still than she could remember being since that far-gone afternoon at the river when she had thought of Jamie's hands on her letter, thought of them as she hung between the sky and the water, disappeared into the sun and the currents.

And then Poe dropped in. He smiled, kissed her. She was actually heartened to see him.

"The editors loved my pictures," he said, somehow making it sound humble by casting his eyes down and using a tone that questioned the validity of the statement even as he uttered it. "I told them it was you who drew out his inner self."

She couldn't even think how to answer, just shook her head. Words had abandoned her. She couldn't use them professionally. And emotionally, she was accosted not by coherent thoughts but by images. She was a parasite, a deer tick sucking on the blood of celebrity, sustaining herself off the achievement of others. The pictures rose up surrealistically—a tick, Heather's stricken face, Georgia's wedding ring, her mother's hands, her father's shadow falling over her, Jamie by firelight, Jamie in the spotlight, just Jamie . . .

"I brought you a gift," Poe said. He took out an enlargement of a fire tower view—all green and soft. There was Prosperity in the distance. Home.

She looked at it through sudden tears that surprised even her. "Thank you," she said.

"You have a good heart," Poe said.

"I do?" she asked in a way that said she didn't believe him, couldn't trust him that far.

"You just don't pay enough attention to it," he said, and then he left without words, only smiling as though he had bequeathed her a portion of the serenity he earned walking between TriBeCa and Rockefeller Center, chanting, meditating, believing.

Poe hadn't been gone ten minutes when Logan came in to find Tess staring at the Ozark vista. He carried another of Poe's photographs, which he taped with ceremony above her computer terminal. It was Jamie, smiling out of Buck Campbell's guise. The Triumvirate had chosen Jamie for the cover.

"Try that for inspiration," Logan said. But his tone was more subdued than usual, gentle even. *He must be scared of me,* she thought, *scared of seeing me like this, vulnerable. He must see me as a woman, not a writer.*

Just thinking it made her cry. It wasn't the appropriate New York response, but then she seemed to have lost her ability to sculpt her reactions. Logan pulled a chair up to face her, put his hand on her knee.

"I didn't think you had it in you," he teased with a tenderness that reminded her of their early days when they had cajoled each other through the worst of times. He would throw a beer bottle at her because an editor had demanded the impossible at an impossible hour, and she would pick it up, finish off what beer hadn't spewed out, and then grin. He'd grin then, too, and hug her. One late night, he had even followed her into the women's rest room and watched as she furiously splashed her face with cold water, fighting back hot tears, swallowing them, not letting them come out for anything. Now here she was, sitting calmly in her office with tears streaming down her cheeks, unashamed.

"I'm not cut out for this," she said.

"This is your life, hon. Whatever's going on with you, it'll pass."

"No, it won't, Logan. I don't want it to."

"I've known you since you first came to New York, since you still had grosgrain bows in your hair. You're tough. It'll pass."

She looked out the window. "I never wore bows."

He leaned closer. "What's this about? I'll fix it. More money? More lead time? A new job title? You name it."

She smiled and hooked his index finger with hers. "Someday," she said, "I'll tell you a story."

"First, could you write me one?"

Tess tried. She strung together the facts as Georgia had recited them. She wrote it off the top of her brain, letting nothing penetrate deeper. She wrote fiction.

The editors hated it. They kept calling for rewrites, plaguing her with their questions and sprinkling comments in bold typefaces throughout the columns of her prose. "Punch it up here," they said. "We need a more naked sense of him. He's hiding behind that wife." They raged about the impending *People* magazine cover, infuriated by the possibility of being scooped. They cited Poe, who had, they pointed out, spoken in curlicue praise about her touch with Buck Campbell, how she had kindled something in him. And there were the pictures to prove it, the star's eyes blazing with some fire, some unexplained fire. Why couldn't she explain it in the article? Why couldn't she, *wouldn't* she, do with the story what she had done with him in person? This obstinacy wasn't like her.

Despite the pressure of having the editors gather around her computer, breathing their hot Scotch breath down her neck, Tess just couldn't bring herself to write even the outlines, the sexy outlines that her editors so often mistook for substance because she had a talent for fleshing it out with her own observations. The editors only wanted surface really, whatever had sex appeal and lust value, whatever would sell magazines. She was sorry they would sell magazines off that look in Jamie's eyes on the cover. She was sorry that the passion she and Jamie shared would make Buck Campbell fans pause in the supermarket, make them buy the magazine and in turn more records, fueling him ever upward. It hurt her to see what she and Jamie shared exploited on newsstands and in record stores. But there was nothing she could do about it. It had gone too far and already belonged to these editors and to a professional code, to the editorial process that had paid for her luxury apartment and her J. Peterman clothes and her long vacation days on Greek islands.

They left her, closed her door behind them, left her alone. Tess felt exhausted by the ordeal, by the ordeal of her goals and her achievement and her aloneness. She could only identify her fatigue as being sick of always exploiting the surface of things. She wanted to go deeper, find some way to write that would help, do some good. She wanted her writing to be like an Ozark creek, so clear on the surface that you only saw the stones gleaming like tiger's-eye in the depths. This surface career wasn't what she had sacrificed Jamie for, what her Pop had sacrificed his happiness, his marriage, his life for. When she had longed to write, it had not been a longing to spend her days chasing stars. This is not what she had dreamed of when, as a girl, she had lain awake at night with aspiration schussing through her. Then, she had wanted to lay bare the wondrous ways that one person was connected to another and to explore in print the intricacies of the natural world. She had wanted her writing to *mean* something.

The office was deserted. For once, everyone had gone. There was a big premiere tonight. Brad

Pitt was scheduled to appear. Sandra Bullock, maybe. Tess floated in the absence of everyone, staring up at Jamie, seeing the love in his eyes for her. And after some time, her hands found the keyboard. She began to write.

CHAPTER TWENTY-TWO

Tess walked home. It was late, but the streets of the city still coursed with people: Young men in khakis exercising their dogs or their toddlers. Teenagers moving en masse. Beautiful women blithely wearing cashmere shawls and Mets caps and high-top tennis shoes. Tess loved them all now as she had loved them her first summer, all seeming to possess themselves and their path on this sidewalk.

She paused on the cobbled corridor behind the Museum of Natural History. Fireflies were flickering there, and it was her habit to stop and watch them and to remember. Though now she couldn't find the past. There was only this moment as it existed for her and as she imagined it existing for him. She could imagine Jamie imagining her, holding her whole in his mind. It made it more real, somehow, that he could see her doing this, that he could this very moment be flying between Hong Kong and Singapore while in his mind he saw Tess this way, standing here looking at the lightning bugs and thinking of home. She felt the way she had felt as a child when she had stayed for long strokes underwater, where she believed God could see her, God alone.

She had given Jamie eyes to see her. He was the only one in the world who could see into her life, into her heart. He was the only one she had allowed, ever. Pop could never have understood her, not understood her to have fears. She had struggled to summon courage—first as a student struggling to approach a professor at college for help, and later, as a fledgling reporter, forcing herself to interview her first college president, then mayor, then governor. But Pop had applauded her, thought her brave. He often bragged to others about her fearlessness. He was not much comfort because he believed so blindly in her strength, her intellect, her drive: his bright girl. She had never disappointed him. She had taken off, at first propelled by the fear of disillusioning Pop. But then, after he was gone, it was fear of crashing. There was no safety net, not even the cushioning effect of his belief in her anymore. With Pop's death, Tess truly had been a woman with no place to go but up. Wings were all she had. No father, a mother who had retreated, a love who had evaporated at her command. There was no one to catch her if she fell. She was haunted by that. During the early days in New York, before she had made any sort of friends, she used to lie in her bed—panic cacophonous inside her—and think, *Nobody can see me now. Nobody knows where I am. If I woke up dead, nobody would find me. I am alone.*

True, it had been years since the panic had been loud. Tess had walked the streets and seen the other people around her, seen how alone they were and yet how apparently complete. Sometimes New York had seemed a place where eight million individuals orbited around each other, never coming together, never touching really. Everyone floating loose in the universe, not belonging, found his or her way to New York. It was somehow not a choice. It was easier to be alone here, alone and yet not lonely. New Yorkers passed affection to each other. Walt Whitman had described it long ago as, "O Manhattan, your frequent and swift flash of eyes offering me love. . . ."

Within the city's labyrinthine passages, Tess had constructed her own small town, her own home. In June, she could stroll this walk behind the Museum of Natural History and watch the lightning bugs flicker as they had in her backyard in Prosperity. When the snow was flying, she could hike on the rocks around the Central Park lake and project herself onto Ozark stone. A few times she had taken a cab up to Harlem and eaten at Sylvia's, eaten fried chicken and stewed greens and mashed potatoes with a pool of melted butter: Soul food. Home-cooked food. Arkansas food. Food for her soul. She sometimes went inside the museum and stood in front of the exhibit that depicted the landscape of the Ozark Mountains. She stood for hours, a portrait of herself reflected in the glass. She stared at her reflection, at the trees and stuffed game beyond it. She saw herself superimposed over a picture of home; she saw herself home.

Her rituals had been enough to make her believe that she belonged someplace, that there was a swath of the Upper West Side that was mapped out in her imagination as home, even if everyone around her was moving along their own plane, guided by another map entirely, one that overlaid hers without contradicting it. She

142

thought of New York as one of those interweaving maps in an encyclopedia. And each life, such as her own, was a single piece of plastic with a course mapped out on it. It was laid down over all the others, intermingling, but if you peeled any one of them away, it revealed that none of the courses ever intersected. Everyone was alone in a crowd.

Noting all this, she had grown more comfortable with her aloneness, would have even claimed to treasure it. Certainly, her solitude had served as excuse many times, something so dear she wasn't willing to relinquish it to any sustained intimacy. But dwelling comfortably in aloneness is a different thing from being happy. It can be serenity. But it rarely, for Tess, could be called happiness.

But now the serenity was somehow vanquished. Jamie could see into the hours and movements that made up her existence. She was not alone anymore, and the home she had charted out of reflected glass and museum exhibits and rocks in the park no longer sufficed. She could see the artifice. Walking home from work up Columbus like this was just walking up Columbus, not a summer night with lightning bugs in her backyard by the creek. She couldn't conspire any longer with New York to make it home. Her life echoed off the bluffs of her memory. It was all space, no boundaries, no safe walls. She was homeless, cast out by a homecoming. She had stepped into another lifetime. She could not return to what she had deluded herself with here, to what she had constructed into a version of home.

Could Jamie? She mulled Jamie's life. Sometimes, these last days, he had left his fuzzy voice

143

on her machine from across the Pacific: "*Tessie, it's me. I'm thinking about how far apart we are, but how I still feel like we're home.*" Or he'd just say, "*Hey, are the stars out tonight?*"

She never answered the phone anymore, always let the machine pick it up. If she spoke to him now, she didn't know how she could ever hang up and break the connection. She didn't know how she could ever give him up again.

CHAPTER TWENTY-THREE

Logan called the next morning after he read the story she had left on his desk with a note that said, *I hope this explains why I can't do this cover story.*

"Why didn't you tell me?" he asked.

"It's personal."

"Girl, I've seen you so upset that you actually ate a brownie with ants crawling all over it. And you can't tell me something like this because it's *personal?*"

"I brushed the ants off, Logan."

"This is the story," he said. "It's beautiful."

"That's for you. No one else."

"But . . ."

"Do this for me," she whispered.

Later that day, she went into the office, and she quit. She told Logan, then the managing editor, that she was leaving. She didn't do it with any heat. It had been coming for a long time, this wish to disentangle herself, to find something real for herself. Now her time with Jamie pulsed inside her as a beacon of what she was missing and what she should at least go out looking for. So she quit, even refused to make the scheduled trip to London to interview Hugh Grant. She just couldn't.

In the quiet that followed, she reread *Jane Eyre* and ate chocolate sorbet. Federal Express buzzed her one day, and it was a package from Jamie, a tape with some new songs he'd written, a T-shirt with his backside plastered all over it—and the words in Japanese. She slept in it. She listened to the tape on her Walkman as she circled the park, walked up and down Broadway. He sang to her again.

One day she passed a newsstand. He was on two magazine covers. She picked up the copy of *People* magazine: *America's Beloved White-Hat Country Boy Sings His Song Worldwide.* She flipped through the pages. Heather's name was on the piece, but there was no mention of Tess or an ex-husband or any past that Georgia hadn't ordained.

Then she reached for her magazine, for the one with Jamie smiling, his hand over his heart. Inside was a photo essay and a clip job, no news. Poe's pictures were beautiful. Jamie was heartbreaking. And she was free.

So even before she discovered how much her life was going to change, renewed vigor filtered into every cell of her body. She quickened as though once again she had swung out over the swimming hole at Sugar Creek, swung out in the blue air and hung there suspended even in motion and willed herself to let go. Once she hit the water, she was all sensation, all alive, and she rose up out of the rippling pool new, the waves she had made marching away into infinity. That was how she felt now.

A morning came when she simply called up a real estate agent in the Ozarks and flew out. She walked through woods, along water, and found what she wanted in the little rock cottage clinging to a hillside above Sugar Creek. It needed work, of course, but dogwoods grew around it and maples and oaks. She sat on the porch and listened to the pines hushing each other in the high breezes of summer. The cottage was secluded. Here, she could write and send her work whizzing by her PowerBook's modem to any point on earth that was equipped with a fax machine. Here, she could write below the surface, write all the new stories that had yet to happen to her.

Tess got down on her knees and polished the wood floors until she could see her face in them. She hung her great-granny's quilt out on the line and brought it in, smelling of sunshine, and spread it on her bed. She cut lilacs and kept them in a Mason jar on her nightstand so that when she woke in the night, their scent was like a presence in the room. She lingered on the porch swing and ate ice cream and watched the fireflies rise like mist from the grass.

When she went back to New York for the last time, to give up her apartment and box up what belongings would fit in her new life, her friends gave her a bemused farewell party. They promised to buy Timberland boots and come visit her in the hills. Logan placed a bet on how long she would last. But she knew better. She knew that she had money saved, wood to burn, fields to walk. And she knew she would have company.

CHAPTER TWENTY-FOUR

The baby was born when February howled around the Ozark mountain like wolves. The snow was drifted on the north side of the cottage, but smoke was curling out of the chimney. Her cousin Lou came over to keep the fire stirred and to make a pot of chicken and dumplings. The midwife was kind, a new friend who had given up life in Seattle to move back to her roots. She and Tess had immediately recognized each other, though they had never met.

The birth unfolded during a snowstorm. And after everyone had gone, Tess moved slowly around the room, the pine floor creaking, with the baby in her arms. She had never doubted that this baby was right. She had known from the beginning that it was the way forward and the way back. It answered all her old questions and urged her to ask new ones. She sat in the rocker as the gray day evolved into an evening that was cobalt in the brightness of the snow. The only music in the hush of the storm was a homemade tape of Jamie singing love songs. He had sung them like lullabies: *Remember me by firelight, wake to me at dawn. I'm faithful as the mountain, clear and certain as the creek. Think of me in sunshine, plant me flowers by the porch. Forget-me-nots. I'm always there. Forget me not.*

His voice hummed through the house, through

Tess who loved him, through their sleeping child. *You're the moon that moves my ocean, the stars that lead me home. You're the dogwoods in the springtime, and the winds that blow at night. You're the fireflies in the summer and the flowers by the porch.*

She felt safe in the shelter he had built for her when they were nothing more than kids celebrating a football game on a moonlit creekbank, when he had lifted her off the ground and given her wings with his love. All her time away and alone, she had longed for this homecoming, yearned to dwell again in the rooms of his song. *Forget-me-nots. I'm always there. Forget me not.* His song was, had always been, a place her size— more vast than any small town or any city, yet cozy too as this rock cottage where even now the fire stirred and murmured in the stove.

She heard his footsteps on the porch, watched the doorknob turn. He filled the doorway, snow blowing around him in the porchlight. Then he was kneeling beside her where she could look full into the face he had brought her. She smiled through her tears, he through his. He kissed her forehead, her eyelids. He touched her lips, with his.

The baby squirmed in her arms, batted his little fists, cooing. Jamie stroked his son's fine hair, and the baby wrapped a hand around his father's least finger. "Look who's here," Tess whispered, gazing at the new downy face.

The baby looked up at them then, his eyes gray as the road that takes you home.

IF YOU HAVE ENJOYED READING
THIS LARGE PRINT BOOK AND
YOU WOULD LIKE MORE
INFORMATION ON HOW TO
ORDER A WHEELER LARGE PRINT
BOOK, PLEASE WRITE TO:

WHEELER PUBLISHING, INC.
P.O. BOX 531
ACCORD, MA 02018-0531